FUNNY STORIES
TO READ OR TELL

FUNNY STORIES
TO READ OR TELL

compiled by

Mildred Corell Luckhardt

Illustrations by

Ralph J. McDonald

Abingdon

Nashville

Library of Congress Cataloging in Publication Data
LUCKHARDT, MILDRED MADELEINE (CORELL) 1898-
comp.
    Funny stories to read or tell. CONTENTS: Credle,
E. The pudding that broke up the preaching.—Lester,
J. Mr. Rabbit and Mr. Bear.—Kelsey, A. G. The
donkey goes to market. [etc.]
    1. Children's stories. [1. Short stories. 2. Humorous
stories] I. Title.
PZ5.L965Fu   813'.008 [Fic]   73-5984

ISBN 0-687-13869-8

THE COMPILER AND PUBLISHERS WISH TO THANK INDIVIDUALS AND PUBLISHERS FOR THEIR
PERMISSION TO USE COPYRIGHTED MATERIAL AS FOLLOWS:

Brandt & Brandt, New York, and Curtis Brown, Ltd., London, for "A Model Letter to
a Friend" and "Wednesday Madness" from *Penrod—His Complete Story* by Booth
Tarkington. Copyright © 1914, 1915, 1916 by International Magazine Company. Copyright renewed 1942, 1943, 1945 by Booth Tarkington. Reprinted by permission of
Brandt & Brandt and of Curtis Brown, Ltd.

The Dial Press, Julius Lester, and the Ronald Hobbs Literary Agency for "Mr. Rabbit
and Mr. Bear" from *The Knee-High Man and Other Tales* by Julius Lester, illustrations by Ralph Pinto. Text copyright © 1972 by Julius Lester. Reprinted by permission of The Dial Press. British rights granted by the Author and the Ronald Hobbs
Literary Agency.

Harcourt Brace Jovanovich, Inc., for "The Recital" (retitled "Flutes and Scratchy
Wigs") from *Fripsey Fun* by Madye Lee Chastain, copyright 1955 by Harcourt Brace
Jovanovich, Inc., and reprinted with their permission.

Harcourt Brace Jovanovich, Inc., New York, and The Bodley Head, London, for "The
Recital" (retitled "The Organ Recital") from *The Middle Moffat* by Eleanor Estes.
Copyright 1942, 1970 by Eleanor Estes. Reprinted by permission of Harcourt Brace
Jovanovich, Inc., and The Bodley Head.

Harper & Row, Publishers, for "The Skunk in Tante Odette's Oven" from *The Talking
Cat and Other Stories of French Canada* by Natalie Savage Carlson. Copyright, 1952
by Natalie Savage Carlson. Reprinted by permission of Harper & Row, Publishers.

Marion Holland for "Billy and Fats Camp Out," "Fats Takes the Cake," and "Fats
Wins a Prize" by Marion Holland, which first appeared in *Story Parade*, copyright
1953, 1954, 1952 respectively. Rights assigned to Marion Holland in 1955. Reprinted
by permission of the author.

Holt, Rinehart and Winston, Inc., and McIntosh and Otis, Inc., for "The Lass That Couldn't Be Frighted" from the book *Heather and Broom* by Sorche Nic Leodhas. Reprinted by arrangement with Holt, Rinehart and Winston, Inc. and McIntosh and Otis, Inc. Copyright © 1960 by Leclaire G. Alger.

Alfred A. Knopf, Inc., for "Santa Claus Knows" copyright 1949 by Marion Holland. Reprinted from *Billy Had a System* by Marion Holland, by permission of Alfred A. Knopf, Inc.

David McKay Co. for "The Donkey Goes to Market" copyright 1954 by A. G. Kelsey. From the book *Once the Hodja* published by Longmans Green & Co. Reprinted by permission of David McKay Co.

Thomas Nelson, Inc., for "The Pudding That Broke Up the Preaching" from *Tall Tales from the High Hills* by Ellis Credle, copyright © 1957 by Ellis Credle. Reprinted by permission of the publisher, Thomas Nelson, Inc.

Western Publishing Company, Inc., for "Zip and the Alarming Clock" by William O. Steele, from *Story Parade*, copyright 1952 by Story Parade, Inc. Reprinted by permission of Western Publishing Company, Inc.

MANUFACTURED BY THE PARTHENON PRESS AT
NASHVILLE, TENNESSEE, UNITED STATES OF AMERICA

To George William and his sisters and cousins and to all the girls and boys, and grown-ups, who have asked for "stories that will make us laugh"; and to the many librarians and teachers who have helped me find such stories for this book.

FUNNY STORIES
TO READ OR TELL

CONTENTS

How to Have More Fun with This Book

Do you like to laugh? And listen to other people laughing together because you have made them happy? Do you like to see happy faces?

"Funny stories to read or tell" were selected for this book because of hundreds of girls and boys, from early grades through junior high, in many schools in a number of states. When I talked with them about my books and asked what kind of stories they would like in my next book, they said, "Something to make us laugh," or "Something to make us happy." So I got very busy trying to gather some really funny stories—and here's the book. To each of you who gave me the idea for such a book I say, "Thank you. I hope you'll enjoy this book that you suggested." And to those of you who were not among the many who asked for a book like this I say, "I hope these stories will give you and your friends some happy hours. Perhaps some day you and I may talk together about books."

Grown-ups too have told me they like stories that make them laugh; and I think most of these stories will bring laughs to people of all ages. One famous writer, James Stephens, has said, "Laughter is the health of the mind." Another well-known storyteller and writer, Mary Gould Davis, whom I was fortunate enough to have for a teacher in college, declared that humor gives people a sense of proportion. So, no matter what age you are, whenever you enjoy and share well-written, humorous

13

stories, you are adding to the world's treasure of good health and well-balanced lives.

Here are some suggestions of ways to enjoy this book:

1. Read the stories to yourself. Everyone needs a happy, quiet time.

2. Read or tell these stories to other people: to the younger children in your family, or to those with whom you are baby-sitting; to sick persons or those who cannot see well enough to read; to your Scout troop, or to a group at camp, or in a playground or library. Read them to all sorts of people who will enjoy remembering these stories, and, perhaps, will tell them to other people.

3. Another way to enjoy these stories is becoming very popular. This is in a quickly planned, informal Readers' Theater, in which several people read together, taking the different parts. This idea is spreading fast among girls and boys, and grown-ups, too, in schools, libraries, Scout troops, camps, families, even at birthday parties where people get together for a good time.

You may enjoy Readers' Theater with only a few minutes' preparation, and no scenery or props. Usually there are several copies of the book from which to read; often two or three persons share a book. If you have only one book, make extra copies, in advance, of the story to be read. Or, just before you read it to the audience, each reader might write down a copy as the story is read to those who will take part.

Be sure the waiting audience does not hear your planning session. You may have a big audience or only one or two persons. Perhaps you will read to each other, with no further audience. But this is fun, too.

For example, let's take the first story in this book, "The Pud-

14

ding That Broke Up the Preaching." Choose the narrator, who tells the story. This should be a lively, good reader who can dramatize or "ham it up"—but not too much, of course. The first time, you might decide to have a teacher or librarian as narrator, to keep the story moving quickly so that the people reading the other parts don't get slowed up. Then look over the story together and select the characters: Ma, Saphronie, Hitty, Lucy, Sally, Rufus, Pa, and the good-natured but unfortunate preacher.

For about ten minutes or less go over the story together so each understands his or her part and can read it in a slow, fast, loud, or whining manner, or in any other way that fits the part. Now you are ready for your audience. The narrator announces the story's title, then begins, "Talk about puddings . . ." and continues until ". . . Ma called out to her eldest girl." Immediately the one taking Ma's part calls, "Saphronie! I forgot the salt in the pudding . . ." and keeps talking until ". . . big pinch of salt."

Saphronie answers, somewhat out of breath from ironing fast, "Lawsy, Ma," and reads on, ending, ". . . iron'll get all cold."

The narrator reads on, "And she went on ironing as hard as she could." Then Ma shouts, "Hitty, you run in the kitchen and put some salt in the pudding for me," and the narrator reads, "hollered Ma to the next oldest girl." Hitty answers, and the story goes on, with the narrator reading between speakers and giving the cue for each part. The voices will be different, and each person, silently reading along with the narrator, usually becomes the person whose part he or she is reading.

This kind of Readers' Theater is great, for you don't need to spend time rehearsing. In many schools where I have suggested

15

it, the girls and boys have not even read the story once before-hand, but have just offered to take the parts of the characters involved. So, actually, the reading may be done with no preparation at all, apart from choosing the readers. And you can't forget your lines, because they are right before you.

Even slow readers have fun in this way, because they have only a line here and there to read and they forget themselves in taking part. At the same time, though, they are reading along silently with the narrator without struggling with each word.

The first time I tried this kind of Readers' Theater was with a sixth-grade class in Milton School, Rye, New York. I asked if they would be willing to try an experiment with me. None of us knew much about Readers' Theater and, of course, did not know how our attempt would turn out. But we all were willing to try—succeed or fail. So I outlined what we would do. I was to be the narrator, and Mrs. Claire Barron, the school librarian, selected people to play the characters. They were going to read a story from my book *Spring World*, *Awake* and were given seven minutes to go to the other end of the library and read over the story with Mrs. Barron. Meanwhile, the girls and boys who would be the audience talked with me about some of my books.

Seven minutes later the readers came back. We all wondered how our experiment would turn out. I began to read the story, and could hardly believe my ears when each reader picked up his or her part. Some whispered, as they were supposed to do: some called out, just right; each one read just right, with no prompting. The audience was fascinated!

When the first story ended, *everybody* clapped—the audience, the readers, Mrs. Barron, her assistant, Mrs. Lucille Haegele, and I. We were all delighted with the success of our experiment!

16

The readers asked eagerly, "May we do it again?" The audience said, *"We* want to do it now."

Unfortunately there was no more time; but Mrs. Barron promised they would do it again later on with other stories. When the next class came in we tried the Readers' Theater with them, too. Everyone had just as much fun. One girl told me afterwards, "I thought I was a slow reader, but now I find I'm not; and I won't be so afraid to read. It was such fun that I forgot I was reading and just took my part. And all the time I was reading the rest of the story silently along with you. I want to do this often." She had been sharing a book with two others and felt she was reading just as well as they were.

When it was time to go home, the librarian and her assistant told me, "This is the happiest Friday afternoon we have had in a long, long time." The girls and boys who heard them said, "That's right!" They asked me to come back soon for more Readers' Theater. We made a date for after my *Spooky Tales* book was published. Then I was invited in advance to do Readers' Theater with them as soon as *Funny Stories to Read or Tell* became a book.

Meanwhile, though, word of our Readers' Theater experiment spread as those students told their families and their friends in other schools. Soon teachers and librarians in various places asked me to introduce it to their girls and boys. Recreation and Scout leaders, also, wanted to know how to get it started. So did some remedial-reading teachers; and I have been asked to talk about it to teachers' groups, in library schools, and to several library systems.

Although the stories in this book are suitable for Readers' Theater, each story was chosen first and foremost to make you

17

happy. One high school boy, when he heard what kind of book this would be, said to me, "Oh! A happy book! We surely do need more happy books." Each of these stories will make you laugh; and the stories are of great variety, from many different places. You may prefer to enjoy them by yourself instead of in a group; and then you may want to tell them to others. In whatever way you use this book, *have fun.*

People everywhere, in this country and in other countries, are finding out once more what fun storytelling and story-reading to others can be. After finishing this book you may want to join in the fun and learn more about this ancient art, which is becoming so very popular again. Since beginning to collect stories for this book, I have had the privilege of teaching, with Anne Izard, Children's Specialist, courses in storytelling and folk tales sponsored by the Westchester County Library System. Every time we finish a course, more people ask for another one.

It really is surprising how many people of all ages are interested. In some schools, beginning in sixth grade and continuing through high school, classes in storytelling are being held in connection with oral English. Do you have such classes in your school? If not, why not suggest the idea to your teacher?

Some colleges have asked for help from the library system in beginning such classes with students in English and Education.

Since most persons interested in increasing their knowledge and enjoyment of this skill like to know of more books about it, some are listed at the end of the book, along with some collections of stories. Enjoy discovering and using them.

Rye, New York   Mildred Corell Luckhardt

The Pudding That
Broke Up the Preaching

Talk about puddings! There never was a more astonishing one than the pudding Ma Tolliver beat up for the all-day preaching that went on down in Possum Hollow Church on Thanksgiving Day. Folks came down to preachings from all over the countryside in those days. They brought their dinners with 'em, and between sermons and singing that went on morning and afternoon, they spread their victuals on the ground, picnic fashion, and had a real slapbang good dinner.

Everybody tried to outdo everybody else with their pies and cakes and roast turkey and what not, and Ma Tolliver laid off that Thanksgiving to have a pudding that would top everything else at the preaching. She started on it early Wednesday morning, mixing up her meal and molasses, cutting up peaches and nuts and such fixings to make it extra fancy. After she'd had it on the fire a spell, and she was in the shed picking a turkey, she remembered that she'd forgot to put salt in it.

Now every good cook knows a pudding's not right without a pinch of salt, so Ma called out to her oldest girl. "Saphronie!" she says, "I forgot the salt in the pudding, and I'm out here picking a turkey with my fingers all stuck full of feathers. Run in the kitchen for me and put in a good big pinch of salt."

"Lawsy, Ma, I'm a-ironing my dress for the big doings tomor-

19

row. If I stop now my iron'll get all cold." And she went on ironing as hard as she could.

"Hitty, you run in the kitchen and put some salt in the pudding for me," hollered Ma to the next oldest girl.

"I declare to goodness, Ma, I can't do it. I've just been to the witchwoman to get her to take the warts off my hands, and she's smeared axle grease over both my hands and told me not to wash it off till I saw the evening star over my left shoulder. I can't pick up a pinch of salt with axle grease all over my hands."

By this time Ma was mighty nigh wore out with hollering, but she decided to try once more. "You, Lucy! Can't you run in the kitchen and put some salt in the pudding for me?"

"Golly, Ma, I'm a-lying here in bed with cucumber peelings all over my face a-trying to make my skin clear before tomorrow. I can't get up now!"

"Sally!" Ma shouted to the youngest girl. "Hump yourself into the kitchen and throw some salt in the pudding for me."

"Goodness sakes, Ma, I'm a-working like fire to get my hair rolled up on old stockings, so I'll have curls for the doings tomorrow. I ain't got time to salt the pudding!"

Since there weren't any more girls to ask, Ma hollered at her son, "Rufus, please go in the kitchen and throw a spoonful of salt into the pudding." But Rufus was busy, too.

He was a young fellow, just beginning to cotton to girls and do a little courting. "I swan, Ma," he called back, "I'm all full of bear's grease. Been slicking down my hair with it, and now I'm a-greasing my Sunday-go-to-meeting boots. I can't put any salt in the pudding now!"

By that time all the children were used up, and Ma began to holler at her old man. "Lem, can't you stop whatever you're doing and go put a spoonful of salt in the pudding?"

"Shucks, Ma, I'm a-cleaning my gun for tomorrow. S'posing a fat rabbit ran across the road whilst we're a-going. If my gun wasn't ready, we'd miss a good stew for supper. Got my hands full of gun soot. I can't take care of your pudding now."

"Oh, tarnation!" Ma said to herself, clean out of patience. "I'll do it myself!" So she washed the feathers off her hands,

and into the kitchen she marched. She got a good big pinch of salt, went over to the hearth where the pudding was boiling away in a pot swung over the fire, and threw the salt into it.

Well, after a while Saphronie got her dress all done up, and she got to feeling a little ashamed that she hadn't done what Ma asked her to. So she went over to the salt box, got a big pinch, and threw it into the pudding.

Hitty got to feeling bad about refusing Ma, too. "I reckon I could manage to get some salt in that pudding if I tried," she said. So she went into the kitchen, picked up a spoon with her greasy hands, dipped up a good big dose of salt, and stirred it into the pudding.

Then Lucy, lying back on the bed with her face covered with cucumbers, got to thinking that she hadn't done right, not to help her Ma when she was asked. So she got up, went to the hearth, and put some more salt on the pudding.

No sooner had she got out of the way, than Sally came into the kitchen with her hair done up in knobs all over her head. She got a good-sized pinch of salt and dropped it in the pudding.

Then Rufus got to thinking about it after he'd finished his boots. So into the kitchen he went and dipped up a heaping big spoonful. Being a man, he didn't know much about such things, and he thought you had to put as much salt in a pudding as in a pot of stew.

Pa's conscience got to hurting him, too, and as soon as his gun was all shined up and loaded, he clumped into the kitchen, dipped up a heaping spoonful of salt, and threw it over into the pudding.

At last the pudding was done! Ma took it off the fire. It turned out of the pot as pretty as you please.

"That's as fine a pudding as I ever saw!" Ma said. "With a pudding like that, I might even ask the preachers to have some tomorrow."

"Oh yes, do, Ma!" the girls exclaimed.

The next day was sparkling and sunny. Everybody set off, walking to the church. The preaching went fine. As soon as one preacher was winded, another one got up and took his place. By twelve o'clock they were all knocked out, so they called time out for Thanksgiving dinner.

Well, sir, Ma was so proud of that pudding that, sure enough, she invited all the preachers over to have some. There were four of 'em, so she cut off four huge hunks and told 'em to dig in.

The first one that took a bite looked at Ma with his eyes popping half out of his head.

"You never tasted anything like it, now did you?" Ma asked proudly.

"No, sister, I never did, and that's a fact," the preacher said.

"Go on, don't be bashful, finish it up!" Ma urged, and the poor fellow, not to hurt her feelings, took another bite and gulped it down.

Those four preachers sure proved their kind feelings that day. All four of 'em choked down the pudding without saying a word against it.

After they'd staggered off toward the church, Ma cut some off for herself and passed each of her family a piece. Everyone took a bite and looked up, horrified. Then it came out how each of 'em had gone into the kitchen and salted the pudding.

Ma was mortified. "Too many cooks sure spoilt this pudding!" she said.

They spoilt the preaching, too, you can be sure of that. Those preachers didn't save any souls that afternoon. As soon as one of'em would get himself worked up to a hollering pitch, he'd have to stop and whisper for a glass of water. There was so much water hauled up to the pulpit that day that folks stopped thinking about the preaching and began to wonder what the trouble was. Some took to counting glasses.

The Pudding That Broke Up the Preaching

What with preachers plagued with thirst and everybody whispering to each other asking questions, the meeting broke up way ahead of time. The tale about the pudding finally got around, and ever since that time folks around Possum Hollow tell about Ma's pudding that broke up the big Thanksgiving all-day preaching.

—FROM *Tall Tales from the High Hills* BY ELLIS CREDLE

Mr. Rabbit and Mr. Bear

If there was one thing in the world Mr. Rabbit liked, it was lettuce. He would do anything to get lettuce. Well, one day Mr. Rabbit was hopping down the road, and he noticed suddenly that he was passing a field of lettuce. Mr. Rabbit had never seen so much lettuce in all his life. As far as he could see, there were rows and rows and rows and rows of lettuce. And the only thing that stood between Mr. Rabbit and those rows and rows and rows and rows of lettuce was a wire fence.

Mr. Rabbit hopped alongside the fence for a minute trying to decide the best way to get the lettuce. He looked up at the fence and knew that it was too high for him to jump over. He looked down at the ground and for a moment thought about digging a hole and crawling under. But that was too much work. He took a good look at the holes in the wire, but they were too small for him to squeeze through.

"What am I going to do?" said Mr. Rabbit. "I have to have some of that lettuce."

Anybody else would have given up, but not Mr. Rabbit. He went across the road and sat down under a big oak tree to think the situation over. He hadn't been sitting there long before a little girl walked across the road, opened the gate to the field of lettuce, and went inside.

"That's it!" Mr. Rabbit shouted, leaping up. "Tomorrow I'll come here at the same time, and if the little girl comes again, I'll get her to let me in."

The next day Mr. Rabbit was sitting by the gate waiting for the little girl. After a while she came out of the woods.

"Good morning, little girl," said the rabbit, hopping over to her.

"Good morning, Mr. Rabbit."

"The farmer told me to ask you to let me into the field."

"Oh, certainly, Mr. Rabbit," the little girl said. She opened the gate and Mr. Rabbit hopped through.

"Thank you," said Mr. Rabbit. "Now you be sure and come let me out at noon."

"All right, Mr. Rabbit."

Well, Mr. Rabbit hopped to a far corner of the field and began eating. He had never tasted such delicious, scrumptious, crispy, luscious, delectable, exquisite, ambrosial, nectareous, yummy lettuce in aaaaaaall of his life. And he ate and ate and ate and then ate some more. When noon came he was ready to go. He'd eaten so much that it was all he could do to hop to the fence and have the little girl let him out.

But the next day he was waiting outside the gate, ready for another morning of that delicious, scrumptious, crispy, luscious, delectable, exquisite, ambrosial, nectareous, yummy lettuce. Every morning Mr. Rabbit came back and every morning the little girl let him in.

After several weeks the farmer started noticing that a lot of his lettuce was missing. He asked everyone he knew if they knew anything about it, but no one did. So he decided to hide behind a tree and see if he could learn who had been eating his lettuce.

The next morning he was there bright and early, and he saw Mr. Rabbit hop up to the gate. Then he saw his little girl come out of the woods, cross the road, and open the gate to let Mr.

Rabbit into his field of delicious, scrumptious, crispy, luscious, delectable, exquisite, ambrosial, nectareous, yummy lettuce. The farmer was angry, but not at his little girl. He knew that Mr. Rabbit had tricked her, and he was sure angry at the rabbit.

He waited until he was certain that Mr. Rabbit was busy eating lettuce. Then he sneaked into the field.

Mr. Rabbit didn't know that his lettuce-eating days were over. He was too busy enjoying that lettuce. Chomp! Chomp! Chomp! He was eating so fast that he didn't hear the farmer. The first thing he knew someone was holding him by the scruff of the neck, yelling, "I got you, Mr. Rabbit! I got you!" The farmer laughed. "You were trying to eat up all my lettuce. But I got you now! I'm going to teach you a lesson, Mr. Rabbit!"

The farmer took Mr. Rabbit out to a big tree. There he tied a rope around one of his legs and tied the other end of the rope to a limb of the tree. And there was poor Mr. Rabbit, hanging in the middle of the air by one leg, swinging back and forth.

"I'm going to leave you there for a while, Mr. Rabbit. That'll teach you a lesson."

The farmer went away, leaving Mr. Rabbit swinging back and forth, back and forth. Anybody else would've been scared hanging up there in the middle of the air by one leg. But not Mr. Rabbit. He was already busy thinking about how he was going to get down.

He was thinking and thinking and thinking, swinging back and forth. He was thinking so hard that he didn't notice Mr. Bear walking down the road.

Mr. Bear looked up and saw Mr. Rabbit swinging back and forth, back and forth. "Uh . . . Mr. Rabbit?"

Mr. Rabbit was thinking so hard he didn't hear him.

"Mr. Rabbit!" the bear shouted.

"Oh! Hello, Mr. Bear. How're you this morning?" the rabbit said.

"Fine. Fine. How're you, Mr. Rabbit?"

"Oh, just fine. Just fine. I'm taking it easy."

"Mr. Rabbit?"

"What is it, Mr. Bear?"

"Uh . . . could you tell me what you're doing up there?"

"Can't you tell, Mr. Bear?" Mr. Rabbit said. "I'm resting."

"Resting?"

"Yep."

Mr. Bear scratched his head. "Looks to me like you're tied to that limb by one leg."

"That's right, Mr. Bear. And that's the new way of resting."

"It is?" asked Mr. Bear.

"Yes, it is," said Mr. Rabbit. "It's much better than lying down in a bed."

"You wouldn't mind if I tried it, would you, Mr. Rabbit?"

Mr. Rabbit thought for a minute. "Well, I don't know, Mr. Bear."

"Aw, please, Mr. Rabbit."

"Well, all right. But you have to promise not to rest too long, Mr. Bear. I know you. You'll get up here and enjoy it so much that I'll never get to rest again."

"I promise, Mr. Rabbit. I just want to try it for a minute."

"O. K. Take this rope off my leg."

Mr. Bear reached up and took the rope off Mr. Rabbit's leg. Mr. Rabbit jumped down to the ground. Then he helped Mr. Bear put his leg through the rope and pulled the loop tight. "There you are, Mr. Bear. Doesn't that feel good?"

Mr. Bear was swinging back and forth, upside down, but he nodded. "It sure does, Mr. Rabbit."

"Well, I'm going down to the creek to get me a drink of water, Mr. Bear. I'll be back in a few minutes."

"O. K., Mr. Rabbit."

But Mr. Bear never saw Mr. Rabbit again that day. Late that evening when the farmer came back to see if Mr. Rabbit had learned his lesson, he was surprised and angry when he saw Mr. Bear hanging up there instead. But Mr. Rabbit was long gone by that time. All the farmer could do was let Mr. Bear down and hope that he would catch Mr. Rabbit another time.

—FROM *The Knee-High Man and Other Tales* BY JULIUS LESTER

The Donkey Goes to Market

The next story, "The Donkey Goes to Market," is one of many tall tales about a legendary person who has for centuries brought laughter to Turkish girls and boys and men and women. The tales about him began five hundred years ago, when a Turkish schoolmaster was scolding his pupils for some mischief. When he came to a very lively boy, Nasr-ed-Din, he asked, "What did you do?" The boy said that all he did was watch and laugh.

After a moment the teacher said, "As long as the world lasts, people will laugh at you!" And not only in Turkey, but in many other countries, people are still laughing over hundreds of stories about Nasr-ed-Din Hodja. (He added the title Hodja *to his name as a term of respect when he himself became a teacher-priest.)*

Some stories about him are found in the book Once the Hodja *by Alice Geer Kelsey. When you read a Hodja story, you will find some unusual words; but just pronounce them the way they are spelled. And soon you too will be laughing about the Hodja the way Turkish girls and boys do, for laughter sounds the same in any language.*

"I tell you, no! I will not keep this miserable donkey another day!" Nasr-ed-Din Hodja glared at the little gray donkey that was patiently switching off the myriad flies as it waited for the Hodja to fasten on the piece of old rug that served as a saddle.

"A new donkey might be just as stubborn," suggested Fatima, wife of the Hodja.

"This wretch is more than stubborn!" stormed the Hodja. "It eats like an elephant but grows skinnier every day. It is slow as a tortoise, lazy as a pig, mean as a fox, stupid as a fish, and stubborn as a—as a—as a donkey!"

Fatima patted the little donkey, who rubbed its head affectionately against her striped sleeve. Fatima said nothing. She had argued with her husband enough times to know that it was like throwing dry leaves on a fire.

"Say your good-byes to the creature!" Nasr-ed-Din Hodja threw one long leg over the little animal. He made the low throaty "Ughr-r-r-r," which is marching orders to a Turkish donkey. "Next time you see it, someone else will be riding it. You shall see what a fine donkey I shall ride home from the animal market. You know how good I am at buying and selling. I can sell this wretched donkey for enough to buy a fine one, and still have a gold piece left over for you to sew in your headdress."

"Ughr-r-r-r," he whirred to the donkey again. The little animal reluctantly shook its long ears, picked up one tiny hoof, and was off. Gloating over the great bargain he was to strike in the market that day, the Hodja patted the coarse hair of his donkey's neck.

Through the street gate rode the Hodja, and on toward the market place. His long legs dangled at the donkey's sides, his feet sometimes touching the cobblestones of the narrow street. It was hard to pass by the charms of market day, but the Hodja had important business on hand. He nodded to right and to left at his many friends in the market place, but kept straight on until he reached the animal market.

"Here is a donkey that will make some man proud of his bargain," said the Hodja, handing the donkey to the auctioneer.

"Such a good donkey should bring a good price," said the auctioneer. He poked the donkey, pinched its legs, and looked at its teeth. Like the Hodja, he spoke loudly for the benefit of anyone who might be listening.

One after another, the auctioneer led the animals up for sale but not a bid did the Hodja make. His eyes were fixed on one donkey that was bigger, sleeker, and plumper than the others. Surely that was the donkey for him.

Finally, all the donkeys were sold but two—the one Nasr-ed-Din Hodja had brought and the one he had resolved to ride away. He was relieved to see that the auctioneer led up his old donkey first. It would be good to have the money for his sale jingling in his belt with what money he already had, before he started bidding for the beautiful dark donkey on which he had set his heart.

"Here is a donkey worth buying!" The auctioneer rubbed his hands gloatingly as he set the Hodja's old donkey before the little group of buyers. "I have watched this donkey many a time and wished it was mine. See the wise look in its eyes! See the gentle way it holds its head! One look at this donkey shows that it would obey your orders before you gave them!"

Nasr-ed-Din Hodja looked at the donkey's eyes. There was a wise look he had never noticed.

"And look at the muscles," the auctioneer droned on. "What loads it could carry! What hills it could climb! Those slim legs mean speed. I wager this donkey could run faster than any donkey in Ak Shehir!"

The Hodja looked at the donkey's legs. He never had noticed how strong and slim they were.

"See how smooth this donkey's coat is!" said the auctioneer.

"That shows good care. What a pretty shade of gray! What perfectly matching white boots on its feet!"

36

The Hodja squinted thoughtfully at the donkey. It was prettily marked. Strange he never had noticed.

"How much am I offered for the handsomest, strongest, wisest, gentlest, most industrious donkey in Ak Shehir?"

"Fifty ghurush," offered a villager.

Nasr-ed-Din Hodja glared at him. Fifty ghurush for the finest donkey in Ak Shehir, indeed!

"Two liras," called the Hodja.

"Two and a half liras," called a villager.

"Three!" The Hodja held up three fingers.

"Four!"

"Five!"

"Six!"

Up and up went the price until a villager bid ten liras.

"Wait a minute!" called the excited Hodja. He grabbed his money bag from his belt and counted his money. Just what he thought! Ten liras and eleven ghurush.

"Ten liras and five ghurush," called a villager.

"Ten liras and eleven ghurush," shouted the Hodja.

He waited. Silence!

"Only ten liras and eleven ghurush for this wonderful donkey!" exclaimed the auctioneer, who knew perfectly well that was a good price. "Come, someone! Make it eleven liras."

Everyone waited. Silence!

The auctioneer handed the bridle to Nasr-ed-Din Hodja. The Hodja emptied his money bag into the auctioneer's hand. He threw his long legs over the donkey's back and settled into the familiar saddle.

"Ughr-r-r-r," he whirred to the donkey and off they trotted toward home. How proud of his bargaining Fatima would be!

Halfway home he began wondering why he had an empty money bag. He had planned, by good bargaining, to bring home a donkey and more money than he carried away. It was puzzling. Perhaps Fatima could explain.

And perhaps she did.

—FROM *Once the Hodja* BY ALICE GEER KELSEY

The Skunk in Tante Odette's Oven

Once in another time, my friends, an old woman called Tante Odette lived in Canada. She was a plump little woman with beady, black eyes, a pouf of a moustache and a double chin. She lived at the edge of the village in a neat whitewashed house with a sharp roof and two dormer windows.

Tante Odette was all alone except for the beasts in the barn and Chouchou, the big gray cat who lived in the house with her. She worked her own little field and cared for her beasts all by herself because she was too stingy to pay anyone to help her.

For this reason, things did not always go so smoothly for her. The ox broke through the fence or the well froze over or the roof began leaking.

There was that Tuesday morning that she got up very early to start the fire in her outdoor oven. The fat loaves were rising nicely in the pans, the weather was pleasant and there was plenty of dry wood for the fire. It looked like a day in which everything would go right from beginning to end.

Tante Odette gathered a load of wood in her arms and carried it to the oven. She laid it down in a neat pile and picked up a stick. She noticed that the oven door had been left open, so she poked her stick inside to see that no leaves or twigs had blown in. The stick would not go in very far because something was in the way.

The old woman stooped lower and peered into the dark depths of the oven. The sight that met her eyes caused her to scream and slam the door shut.

She went running out of her yard and down the road as fast as her bunions and old bones would take her.

At Albe Roberge's farm, she saw Albe drawing water from the well.

"Albe, Albe," she cried breathlessly, "come quick! There is a skunk in my oven."

Albe let the bucket sink back into the well. He stared at Tante Odette in astonishment.

"Are you sure it is a skunk?" he asked. "Perhaps it is your cat."

"Believe me," said Tante Odette, "if that skunk had turned his weapon on me, you would not have to ask such a question. Of course it is a skunk. Is my Chouchou a black cat with a white stripe down his back?"

Then as Albe still stood there stupidly, she explained the whole matter to him.

"I went out early to start the fire in my oven," she began. "I carried a load of wood in my arms, like this. I laid it down, over here. I picked up this stick, see. The oven door was open so I poke, poked the stick inside, but something was in the way. It was a skunk. A skunk is in my oven."

At last Albe Roberge seemed to understand.

"I will come right over as soon as I draw a bucket of water," he promised.

Tante Odette turned and hurried back to the road. But she did not go home. She headed for the farm of Jean Labadie. If two heads were better than one, three would be even more dependable.

Jean Labadie was on his way to his henhouse with a pail of chicken feed in his hand. Tante Odette panted up to him.

"Jean, Jean Labadie," she cried. "Come quickly! There is a skunk in my oven."

Jean Labadie regarded her politely.

"Are you sure it is a skunk?" he asked. "Perhaps it is a scrap of old fur coat that you threw away."

Tante Odette was becoming quite exasperated with her neighbors. When faced by an emergency, they seemed even more simple-minded than René Ecrette, who went slap, slapping through the fields, talking to the birds and bushes.

"Of course it is a skunk," she insisted. "Would I throw away a scrap of anything? Am I such a spendthrift?"

Jean had to agree that she was anything but a spendthrift.

"I went out early to start the fire for my baking," she went on. "I carried a load of wood in my arms, like this. I laid it down, over here. I picked up this stick, see. The oven door was open so I poke, poked the stick inside. But something was in the way. It was a skunk—in my oven."

Tante Odette moaned and wrung her plump hands.

"I will come over as soon as I have fed the chickens," promised Jean Labadie.

Then the old woman turned and limped toward André Drouillard's farm. The wits of her neighbors seemed unusually dull on this fresh morning that had turned sour so unexpectedly. She would need all the heads she would like to knock together.

André Drouillard was just coming out of his back door. He looked surprised to see Tante Odette calling at such an hour, for the old woman was not given to neighborliness.

"André Drouillard," she wheezed, "come quickly. There is a skunk in my oven."

"Are you sure it is a skunk?" blinked André. "Perhaps you saw a shadow inside as you opened the door."

Tante Odette was outraged.

"Does a shadow have a bushy tail?" she demanded. "Does it have two shiny black eyes? Does it grit its teeth at me? No! I went out early to start the fire in my oven. I carried a load of wood in my arms, like this. I laid it down over here. I picked

43

up this stick, see. The oven door was open so I poke, poked my stick inside, but something was in the way. It was a skunk."

André's face brightened.

"Why didn't you tell me that at first?" he asked. "I will come right over."

So as long as her breath came and went, Tante Odette stumbled from farm to farm seeking help. And everyone came quickly, for although a skunk in one's oven is a calamity, a skunk in the oven of one's neighbor is an interesting diversion. Not since the past Sunday had so many people traveled the dusty road.

Albe Roberge and his family were the first to arrive. Jean Labadie came on their heels. Albe opened the oven door, peered in, then carefully closed it.

"It is a skunk indeed," he said.

Then Jean Labadie opened the door, peered in also, then closed it just as carefully.

"Yes, you are right," he admitted. "It *is* a skunk."

In pairs and threes and fours, the people of the parish arrived. There were five of the blue-eyed Meloches, making jokes with pretty Eulalie Beneteau to make her dimples wink. Henri Dupuis, the storekeeper, who looked as if he had just eaten one of the pickles out of his own crock, was only two skips behind his gossipy wife, Hortense. There was Delphine Langlois, and several others who did not matter and would certainly be of no help.

And each one must look in the oven for himself, close the door and name the uninvited occupant a skunk.

Since everyone who wanted to help had arrived and no one denied that a skunk was in Tante Odette's oven, it was now time to think of some way to get the skunk out.

"I will run home and get my gun," cried Jean Labadie. "I'll put a quick end to that caller."

"No, no," howled Tante Odette, "not in my oven."

"Not in the oven," agreed all the others. "She would not be able to bake bread in it for a month—perhaps never."

"And it would spoil the pelt," added Albe Roberge, who trapped for the trader and knew what he was talking about.

"Perhaps we should get somebody's dog," suggested one of the blue-eyed Meloches. "A dog would bark and frighten him out of the oven."

"No, no," cried Tante Odette, "the skunk must not be frightened while he is in my oven."

Everyone agreed that this was true. A frightened skunk was apt to be a very unpleasant fellow.

"Perhaps we should tie a piece of meat on a string and coax him out," said someone else. "Get a piece of meat, Tante Odette."

"I have no meat," snapped the old woman, "and I wouldn't waste it on a skunk if I had."

So this plan was dropped because no one else cared to use his meat to coax a skunk out of Tante Odette's oven.

"Someone should get the priest," suggested Madame Roberge. "He might know what to do."

But others thought that it was more a matter for Dr. Brisson to take care of.

"He could give him a pill that would put him to sleep," said one, "then we could carry the skunk out into the woods."

"No, no," cried Albe Roberge, "do not let such a fine pelt get away. I will take care of the skunk once he is asleep."

Then the youngest Meloche howled with laughter.

"Ha, ha!" he roared, "and that will be one surprised skunk

45

when he wakes up and finds his skin on Albe Roberge's board and Dr. Brisson's bill in his bare paw."

Then everybody but Tante Odette laughed and a light mood fell upon the crowd. André Drouillard was reminded of the time he had worked in the lumber camps and a porcupine had gotten caught in his boot one night.

"And believe me, my friends," he added, "a porcupine wedged in a boot makes as big a problem as a skunk in an oven."

That promptly set Jean Labadie off on a long tale about a deer that was accidentally shut up in the barn with his cows one winter.

"And when spring came, that doe had twin fawns that I raised with my own calves," he ended.

If old Gabriel Meloche had been there with his fiddle and Tante Odette's bread already baked, the whole thing could have been a gay fete.

Only Tante Odette could not forget the reason that everyone had dropped his work at the start of the morning to hurry to her little farm.

"The skunk!" she reminded them. "The skunk is still in my oven. How can I bake bread today?"

One by one, the neighbors walked over to the oven, opened the door, looked surprised to see the skunk still there, then carefully closed the door again.

"Yes," said each one in turn, "he is still there."

And while this was going on, Samigish the Indian came riding down the road on his sway-backed pony. When he saw all the people in Tante Odette's yard, waiting with the air of those about to sit down to a feast, he dismounted and made his way through the gate.

Tante Odette was overjoyed to see an Indian entering her yard. After all, this was more of a problem for one close to nature.

"Samigish," she cried, "come help us. There is a skunk in my oven. We need your help."

"You sure him skunk?" asked Samigish, who had never heard of a skunk in a white man's oven. Bread or venison or a ham, yes, but never a skunk.

"Of course it's a skunk," said Albe Roberge with disgust, for by this time everyone could see what a foolish question this made.

Samigish opened the door, looked in, then carefully closed the door again.

"What shall we do?" asked Tante Odette.

Samigish licked his lips.

"Young, tender skunk," he said. "Anybody got match?"

"Oh, no, no," screamed Tante Odette, "not in my oven."

Everyone tried at once to explain to the Indian that the skunk was not to be cooked.

Samigish stared at them in puzzlement. He shrugged his shoulders.

"Then why skunk in oven?" he asked.

But he did not wait for an answer. Answers never really explained the white man's queer ways. He mounted his sway-backed pony and rode away without another word.

By now, all the people were becoming a little bored with the skunk matter, and it did not look as if Tante Odette was going to serve any food or drink.

Jean Labadie remembered that he hadn't milked his cows. André Drouillard spoke of the job of cleaning his barn. Madame Roberge said it was long past time for breakfast.

It was at this stage that René Ecrette, the simple son of François, came slap, slapping his feet down the road with his head bobbling about like a loose cork. His dull eyes brightened at sight of the gathering in Tante Odette's yard. Like Samigish, he thought that where there was a crowd of people, there must be food. He turned in.

At the time René entered the yard, Tante Odette was quite at the end of her wits. She made one desperate attempt to do something about the skunk in the oven. This René might be simple-minded, it was true, but it was said that he talked to the birds and the trees. Perhaps he had a way with wild things.

The old woman went running to him, twisting the folds of her apron.

"René," she cried, "René Ecrette. There is a skunk in my oven. Can you get him out without frightening him?"

René nodded his head gravely. And he didn't ask "Are you sure it is a skunk?"

"Then do something," implored Tante Odette.

René nodded again.

"What will you do?" asked Tante Odette.

But René did not answer her. He slap, slapped over to the oven and opened the door. He leaned inside. The people could hear him talking in a low, earnest voice. No one could hear what he said because his head was inside the oven. And no one cared to venture closer to try to hear. There was a tight feeling in the air, and Tante Odette felt it from the knot on top of her head to the bunions on her feet.

At last René stepped back. Everyone stared and stretched his neck. For a few moments nothing happened. Then the sharp face of the skunk appeared in the doorway of the oven. Everyone stepped back a few feet. The skunk clumsily wriggled over the edge and dropped to the ground.

Slowly he started through the yard. The crowd respectfully parted to make a wide path for him—a very, very wide path.

The skunk marched toward the woods. He walked with majesty, his flag of truce held high, and not even Albe Roberge, the trapper, blocked his way. In awe, all watched him disappear in the bushes.

Tante Odette was delighted. The others were amazed. They gathered around René Ecrette.

"How did you get him to come out?" asked André Drouillard.

"What did you say to him?" asked Jean Labadie.

René Ecrette hung his head and swung his arms back and forth because he was not used to such admiring attention from the people of the parish. At last he was persuaded to tell the secret.

"I just told him that if he stayed in the oven any longer," he said, "he would begin to smell like Tante Odette's bread, and none of the other skunks would come near him."

So you see, my friends, only the simple-minded René Ecrette was wise enough to know that even a skunk, the lowliest of beasts, has his self-respect and values the good opinion of his own kind.

—FROM *The Talking Cat and Other Stories of French Canada*
BY NATALIE SAVAGE CARLSON

A Model Letter to a Friend

Every Wednesday, Penrod complained of being sick, and at first his parents let him stay home from school. But when they realized he was "sick" so he wouldn't have to go to school, his father made him stay in bed until next day. That cured Penrod for four weeks, but there came a Wednesday when Penrod felt the need to be very sick again because he had not done his homework. Each one in the class had been told to write a model letter to a friend. Even though Penrod had moaned, his father's heart had not softened; and Penrod was dressing himself mournfully for school.

The rest of the family had gone down to breakfast. His older sister Margaret's door stood open. On her desk, he spied a letter she had been writing. He did not stop to see to whom it was addressed; nor realize that it was a private letter for a young man at a distant university. Without stopping to read even one word of it, he hurriedly wrote "Dear Friend" at the top of the page and signed himself at the bottom, "Yours respectfully, Penrod Schofield." Putting it in his English book, he dashed down to breakfast, and gave it no further thought.

Before the letters were handed in Miss Spence, the teacher, asked a few pupils to read theirs. Penrod thought them boring and began to twist a button on his jacket, yawning and daydreaming.

What happened next is told in the book Penrod—His

53

Complete Story *by Booth Tarkington. Here is the rest of the chapter about Penrod's model letter.*

"Penrod!" Miss Spence's searching eye had taken note of the bent head and the twisting button. "Penrod Schofield!"

He came languidly to life. "Ma'am?"

"You may read your letter."

"Yes'm."

And he began to paw clumsily among his books, whereupon Miss Spence's glance fired with suspicion.

"Have you prepared one?" she demanded.

"Yes'm," said Penrod dreamily.

"But you're going to find you forgot to bring it, aren't you?"

"I got it," said Penrod, discovering the paper in his "Principles of English Composition."

"Well, we'll listen to what you've found time to prepare," she said, adding coldly, "for once!"

The frankest pessimism concerning Penrod permeated the whole room; even the eyes of those whose letters had not met with favour turned upon him with obvious assurance that here was every prospect of a performance which would, by comparison, lend a measure of credit to the worst preceding it. But Penrod was unaffected by the general gaze; he rose, still blinking from his lethargy, and in no true sense wholly alive.

He had one idea: to read as rapidly as possible, so as to be done with the task, and he began in a high-pitched monotone, reading with a blind mind and no sense of the significance of the words.

" 'Dear friend,' " he declaimed. " 'You call me beautiful, but I am not really beautiful, and there are times when I doubt if

54

I am even pretty, though perhaps my hair is beautiful, and if it is true that my eyes are like blue stars in heaven—' "

Simultaneously he lost his breath and there burst upon him a perception of the results to which he was being committed by this calamitous reading. And also simultaneous was the outbreak of the class into cachinnations of delight, severely repressed by the perplexed but indignant Miss Spence.

"Go on!" she commanded grimly, when she had restored order.

"Ma'am?" he gulped, looking wretchedly upon the rosy faces all about him.

"Go on with the description of yourself," she said. "We'd like to hear some more about your eyes being like stars in heaven."

Here many of Penrod's little comrades were forced to clasp their faces tightly in both hands; and his dismayed gaze, in refuge, sought the treacherous paper in his hand.

What it beheld there was horrible.

"Proceed!" said Miss Spence.

" 'I—often think,' " he faltered, " 'and a-a tree-more thu-thrills my bein' when I *recall* your last words to me that last—that last—that—' "

"*Go on!*"

" 'That last evening in the moonlight when you—you—you—' "

"Penrod," Miss Spence said dangerously, "you go on, and stop that stammering."

" 'You—you said you would wait for—for years to-to-to-to-' "

"*Penrod!*"

" 'To win me!' " the miserable Penrod managed to gasp. " 'I should not have pre-premitted-permitted you to speak so until we have our—our parents' con-consent; but oh, how sweet it—' "

55

He exhaled a sigh of agony, and then concluded briskly, " 'Yours respectfully, Penrod Schofield.' "

But Miss Spence had at last divined something, for she knew the Schofield family.

"Bring me that letter!" she said.

And the scarlet boy passed forward between rows of mystified but immoderately uplifted children.

Miss Spence herself grew rather pink as she examined the missive and the intensity with which she afterward extended her examination to cover the complete field of Penrod Schofield caused him to find a remote centre of interest whereon to rest his

embarrassed gaze. She let him stand before her throughout a silence, equalled, perhaps, by the tenser pauses during trials for murder, and then, containing herself, she sweepingly gestured him to the pillory—a chair upon the platform, facing the school.

Here he suffered for the unusual term of an hour, with many jocular and cunning eyes constantly upon him; and, when he was released at noon, horrid shouts and shrieks pursued him every step of his homeward way. For his laughter-loving little school-mates spared him not—neither boy nor girl.

"Yay, Penrod!" they shouted. "How's your beautiful hair?" And, "Hi, Penrod! When you goin' to get your parents' con-

sent?" And, "Say, Penrod, how's your tree-mores? Does your tree-mores thrill your bein', Penrod?" And many other facetious inquiries, hard to bear in public.

And when he reached the temporary shelter of his home, he experienced no relief upon finding that Margaret was out for lunch. He was as deeply embittered toward her as toward any other, and, considering her largely responsible for his misfortune, he would have welcomed an opportunity to show her what he thought of her.

How long he was "kept in" after school that afternoon is not a matter of record, but it was long. Before he finally appeared upon the street, he had composed an ample letter on a subject of general interest, namely "School Life," under the supervision of Miss Spence; he had also received some scorching admonitions in respect to honourable behavior regarding other people's letters; and Margaret's had been returned to him with severe instructions to bear it straight to the original owner accompanied by full confession and apology. As a measure of insurance that these things be done, Miss Spence stated definitely her intention to hold a conversation by telephone with Margaret that evening. Altogether, the day had been unusually awful, even for Wednesday.

—ADAPTED BY MILDRED CORELL LUCKHARDT
FROM *Penrod—His Complete Story*
BY BOOTH TARKINGTON

Penrod's Wednesday Madness

(If this story is read or told immediately following "A Model Letter to a Friend," this brief introduction will not be needed.)

Wednesday always was Penrod's worst day each week. And today, Wednesday, he had made a fool of himself before all the class. He had forgotten to write a model letter to a friend, which had been their homework. So, as he dashed off to school he had grabbed a half-finished letter he saw on his older sister Margaret's desk and signed it "Yours respectfully, Penrod Schofield." How was he to know that it was a sort of love letter Margaret had been writing to a young man who wanted to marry her? And how the girls and boys had laughed at him all the way home from school at lunch time, and yelled some of the mushy stuff in the letter! Why had Miss Spence made him read his letter that morning? And then this afternoon she made him stay a long time and write a long letter to an imaginary friend about school life. What a horrible day this Wednesday was! Part of the chapter about it follows, from Booth Tarkington's book Penrod— His Complete Story.

Penrod left the school-house with the heart of an anarchist; he was a bomb, loaded and ticking. As he walked moodily an oft-repeated phrase beat like a tocsin of revolt upon the air: "Daw-gone 'em!" He meant everybody—the universe.

He entered the house, discovered Margaret reading a book in

59

the library, and flung the letter toward her with loathing. "You can take the old thing," he said bitterly. "*I* don't want it!" The next moment he was out of the house.

Across the street, his soured eye fell upon his best friend, Sam Williams, holding converse with Mabel Rorebeck, an attractive member of the Friday Afternoon Dancing Class, that hated organization of which Sam and Penrod were members. Mabel was shy, but Penrod had a vague understanding that Sam considered her beautiful. Sam had never told his love; he was, in fact, sensitive about it.

Sam was sufficiently nervous without any help from Penrod, and it was with horror that he heard his name and Mabel's shrieked with insinuation. "Sam-my and May-bul! Oh, oh!"

Sam started violently. He and Mabel, enraged, looked up and down and everywhere for the invisible but well-known owner of that voice. It came again, in taunting mockery:

"Sammy's mad, and I am glad,
And I know what will please him:
A bottle o' wine to make him shine,
And Mabel Rorebeck to squeeze him!"

"Fresh ole thing!" said Miss Rorebeck. Unreasonably including Sam in her indignation, she tossed her head at him with an effect of scorn and began to walk away.

"Well, Mabel," said Sam, following, "it ain't *my* fault. *I* didn't do anything. It's Penrod."

"I don't care," she began, when the voice was again lifted:
"Oh, oh, oh!
Who's your beau?
Guess *I* know:
Mabel and Sammy, oh, oh, oh!

I caught you!"

Then Mabel deliberately made a face, not at the tree behind which Penrod was lurking, but at the innocent Sam. "You needn't come limpin' after *me*, Sam Williams!" she said. Then she ran away at top speed.

Stung to fury, Sam charged upon the sheltering tree in the Schofields' yard. Ordinarily, Penrod would have fled, keeping his own temper and flinging back jeers. But this was Wednesday, and he was in no mood to run from Sam. He stepped away from the tree, awaiting the onset.

"Well, what you goin' to do so much?" he said.

"Aintcha got any sense!" shouted Sam, flinging himself upon the taunter. The two boys went to the ground together. They hammered, they kicked. Alas, this was a fight! Once more on their feet, they beset each other sorely, dealing many blows. "Got any sense," was repeated many times; also, "Dern ole fool" and "I'll show you."

The peacemaker who appeared on the scene was Penrod's great-uncle Slocum, who had come to call upon Mrs. Schofield. "Boys! Boys! Shame, boys!" he said, but this did not attract any attention. So he felt obliged to separate the former friends. In so doing he intercepted bodily violence and his clothes were pulled around. His hat was no longer on his head and his temper was in a bad way.

"I'll get you, Penrod Schofield," Sam babbled. "Don't you ever dare to speak to me again, long as you live, or I'll whip you worse'n I have this time!"

Penrod squawked. Then failing to reach his enemy, his fury centered on an object which had never done him the slightest harm. Great-uncle Slocum's hat lay on the ground close by. Penrod kicked that hat with such sweep that it rose swiftly on the autumn breeze, passed over the fence and out into the street.

Great-uncle Slocum uttered a scream of anguish and ran forth to its rescue. Sanity had returned to Sam Williams; he was awed by this deed of Penrod's and filled with horror at the thought that he might be held as taking part in it. He fled, pursued as far as the gate by Penrod, and thereafter by Penrod's voice.

"You better run, Sam Williams! You wait till I catch you! You'll see what you get next time! Don't you ever speak to me again as long as you—!"

Here Penrod paused abruptly, for great-uncle Slocum had recovered his hat and was returning toward the gate. After one glance at great-uncle Slocum Penrod did not linger. There are times when even a boy can see that apologies would seem out of place. He ran round the house to the backyard, and let himself out of the back gate.

The sky was gray, and there were hints of coming dusk in the air. As he proceeded up the alley, a hated cry smote his ears. Hateful words from Margaret's letter he had read in school that morning! "Hi, Penrod! How's your tree-mores?" "What makes you think you're only pretty, ole blue stars?" Two grinning schoolboy faces appeared above a high board fence.

Penrod looked about feverishly for a missile. He made mud balls from the surface of the alley and fiercely bombarded the fence. Naturally, hostile mud balls came from behind this barricade. Penrod was outnumbered, and the enemy was behind the fence. Mud balls can be hard as well as soggy. Some that reached Penrod made him grunt. Finally, one struck him in the pit of the stomach, whereupon he clasped himself about the middle silently, and hopped about.

His plight being watched through a knothole, his enemies climbed on the fence and regarded him seriously. "Aw, you're all right, ain't you, old tree-mores?" inquired one.

"I'll *show* you!" bellowed Penrod, recovering his breath. He hurled a fat ball with such effect that his questioner disappeared backward from the fence. Through the gathering dusk the battle continued. It waged hotter as darkness made aim more difficult. Still Penrod would not be driven from the field. He held the back alley against all comers.

In the darkness he could neither see to aim nor to dodge, all the while receiving two for one. He became heavy with mud. No one could have been quite sure what he was meant for. Dinner bells jingled in houses, then from kitchen doors. Voices called boys' names into the darkness. Bells were rung again—and the voices sounded more irritated. They called and called and called.

Thud! went the mud balls. Thud! Thud! Blunk! "Oof!" said Penrod.

Meanwhile, Sam Williams, having dined with his family, slipped out of the kitchen door and quietly betook himself to Schofields' corner. He stationed himself where he could see all avenues of approach to the house, and waited. Twenty minutes went by, and then Sam became suddenly alert, for the arc-light revealed a small, queer-looking figure slowly approaching along the sidewalk. It was brown, shaggy, indefinite in form. It limped and paused to rub itself, and to meditate.

Peculiar as the thing was, Sam had no doubt as to its identity. He advanced. " 'Lo, Penrod," he said cautiously.

Penrod leaned against the fence and tested one knee-joint by swinging his foot, a process evidently painful. He rubbed the left side of his mud covered face. He opened his mouth wide,

moved his lower jaw slightly from side to side, and settled in his own mind as to whether a dislocation had taken place. He examined both shins; and carefully tested his neck-muscles to move his head.

Then he responded somewhat gruffly: " 'Lo!"

"Where you been?" Sam asked eagerly.

"Havin' a mud-fight."

"I guess you did!" Sam exclaimed, in a low voice. "What you goin' to tell your—"

"Oh, nothin'."

"Your sister telephoned to see if I knew where you were," said Sam. "She told me if I saw you before you got home to tell you sumpthing. She said Miss Spence telephoned her, but she said for me to tell you it was all right about that letter. She wasn't going to tell your mother and father on you, so you needn't say anything about it to 'em."

"All right," said Penrod.

"She says you're goin' to be in enough trouble without that," Sam went on. "You're goin' to catch fits about your Uncle Slocum's hat, Penrod."

"Well, I guess I know it."

"And about not comin' home to dinner, too. Your mother telephoned twice to see if you had come in our house. When they see you, you're goin' to get the *dickens*, Penrod!"

Penrod seemed unimpressed, though he was well aware that Sam's prophecy was no unreasonable one. "Well, I guess I know it," he repeated casually and moved slowly toward his own gate.

His friend looked after him as the limping figure fumbled clumsily with bruised fingers at the latch of the gate. "Say, Penrod, how—how do you feel?" There sounded a little solicitude in Sam's voice for his best friend.

"What?"

"Do you feel pretty bad?"

"No," said Penrod. In spite of what awaited him, he spoke the truth. His nerves were rested; his soul was at peace. His Wednesday madness was over.

"No," said Penrod; "I feel bully! Just great!"

—ADAPTED BY MILDRED CORELL LUCKHARDT
FROM *Penrod—His Complete Story*
BY BOOTH TARKINGTON

Flutes and Scratchy Wigs

The Fripsey Fluters were getting nervous about the recital on Saturday night, when they would play their recorders, old-time wooden flutes. They had been practicing hard; and the boys had been complaining just as hard about the eighteenth century costumes the Misses Wardfield had made for them to wear. They were still complaining as the fluters reached the Wardfield house on the night of the dress rehearsal.

When they rang the bell, Miss Clara answered it. She and her sister were also dressed in costumes. "Isn't this fun?" she said. The girls agreed but the boys just grunted. "Well," said Miss Clara, suppressing a smile. "Do come in."

The rehearsal went remarkably well except for a passage in *The British Grenadiers* which was high, difficult for them and tricky in time. They went over it several times. "I think I'll just go through the motions when we get to that part," whispered Marcy.

Patty nodded sympathetically. "I was thinking the same thing. I don't think the audience would notice with all the others playing."

"I just wish we could leave that piece out," said Sue-Sue. "I never can finger it right."

When the rehearsal was over, Miss Clara said, "Did you bring the wigs? I'd like to see how they fit."

"They're what we brought in those shopping bags," said Liz.

They were made over a foundation of horsehair braids in the shape of a skullcap. The cotton was rolled in curls and sewed to the horsehair. "You really did a very good job," complimented Miss Clara. "This part in the back can be plaited into a queue with a black ribbon bow. Like a periwig."

Folly groaned again. "*Ribbon!* Gosh, what was the matter with these eighteenth century fellas, anyway? All this brocade and lace and now *ribbon!*"

"Don't be difficult, Folly—if you can help it," said Liz. "You know very well it was simply the custom of the time."

"What a time!" said Bink.

But Davey was pleased. "Look at me," he said, posing in his white wig. "I look just like Grandpa Higgins!"

At breakfast the next morning, Marcy was discussing the coming recital with her parents and Aunt Partridge. "And you should have seen us all together last night! The costumes are so cute! And Liz did a wonderful job with the wigs."

Dad grinned. "I've got to see this," he said.

"Sounds lovely," said Mother. "I think it is a simply delightful idea and will be a treat for everyone. After all, Mayville has never had anything like this before."

"That's what I'm afraid of," mumbled Dad behind his newspaper.

"Sam Prescott, you stop that," said Mother. "How did the rehearsal go?"

"Just fine. Except, of course, the boys kept complaining about their costumes."

"Hah!" chuckled Dad.

"Sam!" warned Mother.

"Laura's right, Sam," said Aunt Partridge. "This is going to be charming. I've told the ladies in our knitting club and they are all coming."

"And I posted an announcement on the bulletin board at the Mayville Arts and Crafts Club. I think a lot of the members will come," added Mother. "By the way, Sam, did you send the announcement to the Business Men's Club?"

"Oh, yes," replied Dad with a grin. "I didn't dare *not* do it."

"Practically our whole school is coming," said Marcy. "Mr. Baxter said so."

"I hope the hall is big enough," said Dad.

"Miss Letitia says a flute recital like this ought to be intimate."

"Intimate? With five hundred people?" Dad folded his newspaper and rose.

"Oh, I don't think there'll be five hundred people!" Marcy suddenly looked scared.

"You don't know *what* may happen next Saturday night!" said Dad ominously.

Saturday night the weather was dry and crisp.

"Just the kind of an evening to bring folks out," said Miss Clara happily.

She had the Fripsey Fluters gathered together backstage while the audience was filing in and being seated. The recital was being held in the Community Church Hall and now and then Miss Letitia peeked through the velvet curtains. "We really are going to have a crowd!" she whispered.

Davey kept scratching his head. "This wig itches," he complained.

"Don't do that, Davey," said Patty. "You get your wig all askew."

"I can't help it. It itches something terrible!"

"Oh dear. It's the horsehair braid," said Miss Clara.

"You know these things *are* scratchy," said Folly, pushing his wig back and forth.

"Now try not to think of it," said Miss Clara. "Or you'll all begin to feel it."

"Come, take your places, everybody," called Miss Letitia, beckoning to the Fripsey Fluters.

The stage did have atmosphere! The Misses Wardfield had brought their antique straight chairs for the fluters and the old music stand with the candleholders. From somewhere they had secured three other antique carved music stands and three tall standing candelabra. There was a fourth one standing beside Miss Clara's harpsichord. All were fitted with tall ivory candles which were now lighted. The janitor had turned on a very faint spotlight and the effect was soft and delicate.

Miss Clara took her place at the harpsichord. She had on a flower-sprigged silk with deep ecru lace and instead of a wig, her own hair was powdered very white. If she moved her head quickly, a little cloud of powder floated out.

"Davey!" hissed Folly. "Wilt thee leave thee's wig alone!"

"Very funny," whispered Liz. "You'd make *some* Elizabethans!"

"This isn't Elizabethan. It's eighteenth century," Bink informed her.

"*I* know that! I'm talking about all those *thees!*"

"Don't you mean all these *those?*" teased Bink.

Patty and Marcy dissolved into laughter.

"Why art so merry, lass?" Folly inquired of Marcy. "Hast thee's wig gone to thee's head?"

"Avaunt varlet!" said Bink. "Wouldst speak trippingly and trip up our fellow fluter?"

"That's *not* the proper use of *trippingly!*" said Liz, looking annoyed. "Shakespeare says—"

Folly and Bink ignored her. "Hast occurred to thee that our sister is in the way of becoming an authority on Will Shakespeare, of late?"

Bink nodded. "Hast."

"Is everyone ready?" asked Miss Letitia. "Davey, dear, please push your wig on straight. Could you help him, Liz? Thank you, dear. Now!" she signaled for the janitor to open the curtains.

Marcy's heart was pounding so that she could hardly breathe as the velvet curtains swooshed back and exposed all the Fripsey Fluters to the audience. There was a fine burst of applause. Since the lights were so soft, it was quite easy to see into the audience. Marcy looked away quickly. She didn't want to see anyone she knew. She would be that much more nervous!

Miss Letitia addressed the audience. "Welcome to our very first recorder recital. We hope that through this evening's program, you may become introduced to the recorder, which is really the early English wooden flute, and that you will enjoy hearing the old music played by these flutes. We have tried to simulate here the atmosphere of an evening of music in the eighteenth century. A group of friends might gather any evening and play together just as we are going to play for you tonight."

Miss Letitia turned to face the Fripsey Fluters. She whispered, "One-two-three-four-five-six!" and they began *Sellenger's Round.*

Marcy was so scared, with all those people watching, she could barely see the notes and wasn't breathing in the right places at all. She glimpsed Patty's hands shaking so hard her flute was wobbling up and down. Marcy tried to concentrate on the music and pat her foot underneath her long skirt. If she ever lost the place in this piece of music, she'd never catch up again!

They got to the end at last and there was loud applause. Marcy took a deep breath and winked at Patty who was looking a little pale but she was smiling.

Davey, who had been playing his triangle, was scratching his head again. "Davey!" hissed Liz under her breath. He frowned at her and then pushed his wig forward.

"*All in a Garden Green*," murmured Miss Letitia. "One, two, three!"

This went better. How pretty the flutes and harpsichord sounded together! Marcy could hear it better here in the big hall.

They rested while Miss Clara played some selections from Fitzwilliam's *Virginals Book*. Several were very fast and she shook her head as she played, emitting small clouds of white powder.

Bink clapped his hand over his face to hold back a sneeze.

"Oh!" whispered Marcy. "This is going to be just like the soap flakes!"

Folly looked worried, too. He reached up absently and pushed his wig back and forth.

Marcy looked away quickly. He was so comical with his queue sticking out over one ear! As a matter of fact, her own wig was feeling scratchy but she was trying not to think of it. That horsehair braid was so prickly but they hadn't been able to find anything else that would hold its shape as well for the wigs.

"A-choo!" went Folly, his wig flying forward over his eyes. Bink ducked down behind his music stand to hide his laughter as the audience applauded Miss Clara's playing.

"I ought to take this cussed thing off," muttered Folly, shoving his wig back in place.

"You can't do that! It will just call attention to the whole thing!" Liz whispered frantically.

"*The British Grenadiers,*" murmured Miss Letitia. "One, two, three, four!"

The piece moved along very well until it reached that difficult spot Marcy dreaded. She looked very attentively at the music and kept moving her fingers but she didn't breathe into her flute. To her astonishment there was a dead silence except for Davey's drum! Miss Letitia looked quickly around the circle, her eyebrows raised in surprise. Apparently, each one of the Fripsey Fluters had secretly decided to skip this passage, thinking the others would play it. Davey, however, continued to beat his drum, tapping out each measure with his foot. He never listened to the others anyway. When he reached the end of the last line, he stopped. There was a roar of laughter and tremendous applause!

The Misses Wardfield and all the Fripsey Fluters collapsed with laughter, too. Then Miss Letitia made Davey take a bow. The audience gave him another big round of applause. He looked surprised, scratched at his wig again and sat down.

After that, the recital went very well indeed. It seemed that the mishap and ensuing laughter had relaxed everyone. Even the scratchy wigs were forgotten. They played *Drink to Me Only with Thine Eyes* and *Greensleeves* so well that the audience demanded they play them both a second time. All in all, it was quite a success!

"Methinks this was fair fun, after all," said Folly as the curtains closed.

"Aye," agreed Bink. "But 'twould have been better if thee hadn't had so much wig trouble!"

—ADAPTED BY MILDRED CORELL LUCKHARDT
FROM *Fripsey Fun* BY MADYE LEE CHASTAIN

Billy and Fats Camp Out

A grown-up cousin of Billy Kidwell's was getting married, in Chicago, and Billy's parents were planning to take him to the wedding.

"I hate to buy him a new suit just before the beginning of summer," said his mother, "but I'll get it good and big, so it will do for next year."

Billy complained to Fats Martin about it. "Getting all wrapped up in a necktie, in this weather," he said. "Ugh."

"Tough luck," agreed Fats. "Say, why couldn't you stay with me while your Mom and Pop go to this old wedding?" He asked his mother about it, and Mrs. Martin said certainly Billy could stay with Fats for a few days.

So then Billy's mother called up Fats' mother and said she simply wouldn't dream of asking anybody with five children to look after one more. Mrs. Martin said that when you had five already, one more wouldn't make much difference. Besides, Mr. Martin was away on a business trip, so it wouldn't even mean an extra place at the table.

Well, Billy's mother was glad to quit arguing about it. But she felt she ought to do something in return, so she invited Fats over to stay with Billy for the next two days, until she and Mr. Kidwell left for Chicago.

It was a pretty brisk two days, because Mrs. Kidwell was in such a dither getting ready for the wedding.

But finally she got everything packed to go, and the house all slicked up. So Thursday morning they loaded their suitcases into the car and locked up the house. Then they drove Billy and Fats over to the Martins'.

As the car stopped, Mrs. Martin leaned out an upstairs window and waved her hand and called something, but nobody could hear her over the noise of the engine. So Mrs. Kidwell just waved back at her and told Billy not to be any bother. And off the Kidwells drove, to Chicago.

Mrs. Martin went right on waving, which sort of surprised Billy and Fats.

"Stop!" called Mrs. Martin. "Don't come on the porch. I'll be right down."

"What's the matter with the porch?" Billy asked Fats. "Wet paint?"

Mrs. Martin opened the front door. "We're quarantined," she called to them, "so don't come any nearer. The doctor just left, and I've been trying to phone you. Bobby has scarlet fever."

"Gee, that's pretty serious, isn't it?" asked Fats.

"Not so serious now, with all the new drugs they have now. But the quarantine is very strict. If you come in, you can't go out again."

"But gosh, where'll we go?" asked Fats.

"Goodness, I haven't had a chance to think yet," said his mother. "I've been so busy."

"We can go back to my house," offered Billy. "It's locked, but I know how to get in. And we're plenty old enough to take care of ourselves, aren't we, Fats?"

"Sure, if there's anything to eat around the place. Might as well get scarlet fever as starve to death."

"Oh, there's plenty of cans and stuff," said Billy.

"Well, if you can manage, it will be a load off my mind," said Mrs. Martin, "because I'm certainly going to have my hands full the next few days. Phone me every so often and let me know how you're getting along."

So they went back to Billy's house. Billy pried open the pantry window, which had a loose lock, and let Fats in the back door. "Boy, we can do anything we want!" exclaimed Fats.

"Anything at all," agreed Billy. But the funny thing was they couldn't think of anything special they wanted to do. The house seemed awfully quiet and empty.

"Your Mom sure left the place all polished up, didn't she?" remarked Fats, picking up a piece of dried mud that came off his shoe, and looking around for somewhere to put it. But even the wastebaskets were clean and empty.

"She sure did," admitted Billy. "I guess we probably better make up our beds every morning."

"And whatever cooking and eating we do, we better clean up everything right away," said Fats gloomily.

"Hey!" Billy's face lighted up. "We could camp out for a few days! No beds to make. No dishes to wash. Just till my folks get back."

"Say, that's an idea!" exclaimed Fats. "But what'll my mother say?"

"Oh, I wouldn't bother her about it. What's to eat that we can take?"

There was nothing in the icebox but butter, eggs and bacon. They left the eggs, since raw eggs are ticklish things to carry. But there were plenty of cans and jars stacked on shelves in the pantry.

It was too hot to bother with blankets so they took the two canvas hammocks out of the garage that Mr. Kidwell hadn't got around to putting up for the summer yet, and rolled the supplies up in them.

"One apiece to carry," said Fats. "Now, where'll we go?"

"How about the old Burwell farm?" asked Billy. "The house is burned down, but there's the barn in case it rains, and there's a good spring."

"Swell," said Fats. He phoned his mother and asked how Bobby was, and his mother said Bobby was doing fine. Then she asked if he and Billy had found enough to eat, and Fats said yes, they had. Then she told him to be sure not to get the Kidwells' house all messed up, and he said no, they wouldn't, and hung up.

It was a hot, dusty walk, and as soon as they got there, they dumped the hammocks down and got a long drink from the spring. Then they went exploring in the woods. They found a little stream, not deep enough to swim in, exactly, but deep enough to get wet all over in. By the time they got dressed again, they were good and ready for lunch.

They unrolled the supplies, and it turned out that the butter had melted right out of its paper wrappings. It didn't hurt the cans any, but it sure didn't do the hammocks any good. They scraped as much as they could back into the paper and stuck it in the spring to cool off. Then they fried up about half the bacon and dumped a couple of cans of beans in on top of it.

"Boy, this is the life!" exclaimed Fats as they ate right out of the frying pan. "I could stay right here till school starts."

"I could stay here after school starts," said Billy.

They filled up on beans and bacon and spring water. Then

they set up housekeeping. They slung the hammocks between some posts in the barn, and stacked the cans and stuff neatly by the wall, and rinsed out the frying pan and hung it on a nail.

"Nothin' to do and all day to do it in," said Fats, trying out his hammock. Billy dumped him out of it, and they went treasure hunting through the burned down farmhouse. They found part of a metal bedstead and a knife blade with a charred handle and lots and lots of nails. Just the same, it seemed a long while before it was time to build the fire for supper and stick the potatoes in the ashes.

"Now we give 'em plenty of time," said Fats, "so they get black on the outside and good and mealy inside. Then we pile on the butter. Oh man, I can hardly wait."

While they were waiting, it got darker and a cool breeze sprang up. There was a sudden growl of thunder, and the rain simply poured down. Billy and Fats raced for the barn, and stood in the doorway and watched their fire sputter out.

When the rain slowed down to a drizzle, they dug the potatoes out, half-cooked, and ate them that way, because it was too wet to make another fire. Even with a jar of pickles, it wasn't a very fancy meal. The rain had washed a lot of mud into the spring, so they had to go to bed thirsty.

A hammock is mighty comfortable to lounge around in, but after a long while Billy decided that there must be some sort of a trick to sleeping in one. He twisted and wiggled, but still he sagged too much in the middle. He could hear Fats thrashing around in his hammock.

"I wonder how the Navy does it," he said finally.

"Oh, we'll get used to it," grunted Fats. "After a few nights." But he didn't sound very enthusiastic.

There weren't many mosquitoes, but they were all hungry. At last Billy got to sleep with the sides of the hammock pulled over his face. Another thunderstorm in the night woke him up, and

there turned out to be a leak right over his head. He lay down the other way, so the leak was over his feet, but that didn't help much. He was still wide awake when it began to get light.

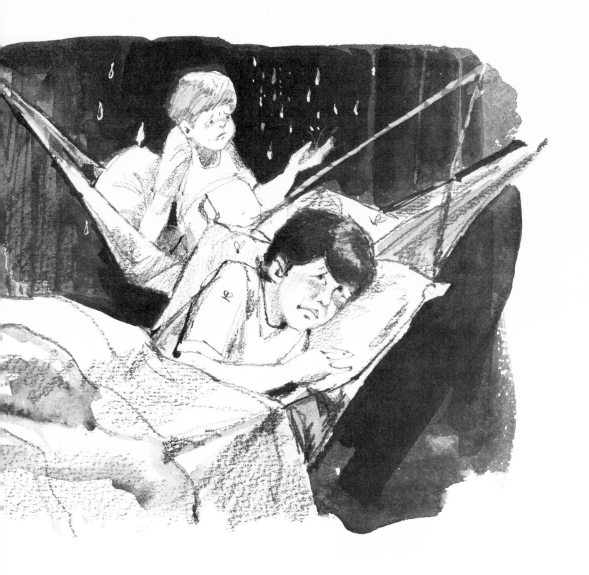

Fats was awake, too. "Boy, have I ever got a crick in my back," he croaked.

"A good hot breakfast will fix us up," said Billy, but all the wood they could find was too wet to burn.

"We could open a can of beans and eat 'em cold," said Fats finally.

Billy just looked at the can and the can opener. "If we went back to my house, we could scramble those eggs we left."

"Sure, sure, we'll come right back," said Fats heartily.

They practically staggered all the way to Billy's house, they were so sleepy. "Gee, I forgot to shut the pantry window," said Billy, as he climbed through.

Fats climbed in after him, and then sniffed the air. "Say, somebody's been smoking a cigar in here," he whispered. "Burglars, I bet! Maybe we better call the police."

"No burglars would stick around in broad daylight," whispered Billy.

They listened for a long time but there wasn't a sound. Then they took a quick look around. Nobody there. Billy opened the silver drawer in the dining room. Nothing seemed to be touched.

"Hey, it wasn't burglars after all!" Fats called from the kitchen. "It was just a tramp. Look here."

Somebody had scrambled all the eggs and made coffee. There were egg shells and coffee grounds in the sink, and an eggy pan on the stove, and a dirty cup and dishes with bits of cold egg and cigar ashes stuck to them, on the table.

"We better have a look around and see if he took anything besides food," said Fats. He stuffed a handfull of dry cornflakes into his mouth, and yawned through the cornflakes.

Billy inspected the box on his mother's bureau where she kept earrings and things, but it looked as full as ever. He went into his own room, and there was Fats, stretched out with his muddy shoes on the bedspread. He was sound asleep and snoring.

It made Billy yawn, just to look at him. He took off his shoes and lay down on the other bed. But the more he thought about the mess in the kitchen, the madder he got. The nerve of that tramp, and after all he and Fats had been through, just to keep the place nice and clean. What if the tramp figured he was onto a good thing and came back for another meal, while he and Fats were asleep!

Billy dragged himself off the bed and staggered down the stairs. He made sure the doors were locked. Then he got out all the pots and pans he could find and stacked them up under the pantry window, balanced on top of each other and very wobbly. There, he thought, I'd like to see any old tramp get in over that without waking us up.

He just barely made it up the stairs again and fell flat on the bed. But it seemed as if he hadn't been asleep five minutes when Fats shook him.

"Hey, that tramp's back again," whispered Fats in his ear.

There was a noise downstairs like somebody kicking a kettle clear across the kitchen.

"Jeepers, just listen to him!" gasped Fats. Words floated up the stairs that Billy and Fats weren't even supposed to know.

"What'll we do?" asked Fats.

"Go right down there and tell him to clean up the kitchen," said Billy, heading for the stairs. Fats followed, a little bit behind, because after all it was Billy's kitchen. But when they got close enough to see into the kitchen it was Fats who rushed right in.

"Gee whiz, Pop!" he exclaimed. "How did you get here?"

Mr. Martin just looked at him, and then sank heavily into a chair.

"Where have you boys been?" he demanded. "Do you know that the police are looking for you all over the county?"

"The police?" gasped Fats. "Why, what have *we* done?"

"That's what I want to know," said his father. "Your mother phoned me about Bobby, and I came right back. Seemed to both of us like a good idea if I came over here and rode herd on you two. Last evening I figured you were at the late movie, but when you didn't show up, I phoned all your friends. Got their parents out of bed in the middle of the night, looking for you. This morning I gave the police your descriptions. Everybody in town knows you're missing, except your mother. *Where have you been?*"

"Why, we just decided to camp out, to keep the house clean," said Billy. "And a tramp busted in and ate all the eggs and made a big mess."

"*I* ate all the eggs," replied Mr. Martin grimly. "Had to come in the window because I didn't want to leave the place unlocked. Stepped into some kind of booby trap and knocked over a can of flour when I fell down. And I know who's going to clean it up, too."

"Us?" asked Fats, in a small voice.

"You," replied his father, walking over to the telephone, and leaving a trail of floury footprints. "I'm going to phone your mother and tell her you're just fine. And *then* I'm going upstairs and go to sleep. Because of you boys, I didn't close my eyes last night."

86

Fats opened his mouth, but he didn't say anything. He just put the dishpan in the sink and started the water running.

"And besides," he said to Billy, "we'll have to lug all that stuff back again. The funny thing is, I can't think of one single thing we did wrong."

Billy plugged in the vacuum cleaner.

"Not one single thing," he agreed, yawning. "It sure is a tough life."

—MARION HOLLAND

Fats Takes the Cake

Billy was invited to Stew Wilson's birthday party, but Fats wasn't.

"Maybe your invitation got lost in the mail," Billy suggested.

"Maybe it didn't," said Fats. "I had a big fight with Stew last week, and we aren't speaking."

"Gee, that's tough. Remember the refreshments at Stew's party last year?"

"I sure do," said Fats.

"Look, why don't you go around to Stew's and make up with him?" asked Billy. "How can I?" Fats demanded indignantly. "I forget what the fight was about."

"What of it? Just go around and say you were wrong."

"I will not!" shouted Fats. "Stew was wrong, and he can come around and make up with me if he wants me at his old party!"

Billy gave up. Some people are so pig-headed that it doesn't even do any good to point out to them how pig-headed they are.

The party turned out to be a scavenger hunt, and not even Stew knew ahead of time what was on the list of things they had to hunt for. But first each boy had to draw a girl's name out of a hat, to see who his partner would be. Stew drew a blank slip, because at the last minute one of the girls couldn't come. So that meant Stew had to go without a partner.

When Billy looked at his slip, and saw Peggy Crowley's name, he got Stew into a corner and offered to trade slips with him.

88

But Stew said no thank you, and what kind of dope did Billy think he was anyway?

Then Stew's mother announced that there would be a prize for everybody that came back with everything on the list, and a grand prize for the couple that got back first. Then she handed around the lists, which were all alike:

Pine cone
1924 penny
garden rake
last Sunday's paper
sock with a hole in it
black cat

Practically everybody grabbed a list and rushed right out and started ringing doorbells.

"Come on," exclaimed Peggy, pulling at Billy's sleeve. "They're all getting ahead of us."

"Let 'em," said Billy, studying the list. "The only tough thing is the black cat."

"I know where to find plenty of cats," said Peggy. "Only not black!"

"Say, I just remembered something!" cried Billy. "Come on!"

He cut through a couple of backyards and dashed up the street to Fats' house.

Fats was sitting on the front steps. "What's the matter?" he asked. "You have a fight with Stew, too?"

"Nope. It's a scavenger hunt, and I got to rustle up a black cat somewhere," explained Billy.

"Well, start rustling. You better hurry, too, because here comes Peggy Crowley," warned Fats.

"Ugh! She's my partner."

"Billy Kidwell, you wait for me," panted Peggy. "Mrs. Wilson said the partners had to stay together."

"Keep up with me, then. Listen, Fats, last spring your kid brother Bobby was trying to give me a black kitten, only my mother wouldn't let me take it."

"I know," said Fats. "Mom wouldn't let us keep it, either."

"Well, where is it now?" asked Billy.

"How should I know? He found somebody to take it, but I don't know who."

"Ask him, can't you?" urged Billy.

"I don't even know where he is. He went out to play right after lunch, and he doesn't have to be back till supper."

Billy groaned. "I need a black cat before then, and I got to find all these other things, too. Say, be a pal and find Bobby and ask him, will you? Then you could get the cat for me, and have it here by the time I get back with the other stuff."

"Sure I could. But why should I?" asked Fats. "I wasn't even invited to this old party."

"Oh, come along, Billy," cried Peggy. "We can find our own black cats."

"Keep your shirt on," said Billy. "Listen, Fats, you get me a black cat, and I'll bring you a piece of cake."

"They'll have ice cream, too," said Fats. "And candy."

"Sure, sure, everything they got," promised Billy.

"Well, okay then. I'll see what I can do." Fats heaved himself up off the steps and went in search of Bobby.

"See, we're doing it the smart way," Billy pointed out to Peggy. "Now all we have to do is dig up the other things and pick up our cat on the way back."

91

"*If* Fats gets a cat," sniffed Peggy.

"What do you mean? *If?* I can count on good old Fats."

They found a pine cone right away, and then they started ringing doorbells and asking for the other things on the list. By the end of one block, they had collected the sock with a hole in it, last Sunday's paper, and a garden rake, and the only thing they had to promise to return was the garden rake.

But it took them a long time, because Peggy kept asking about black cats, although Billy told her about a million times that Fats would have one for them.

Then they started on the next block, still looking for the 1924 penny. It was pretty discouraging, how many pennies everybody had, and the number of different dates on them that weren't 1924. And, of course, Peggy went right on wasting time asking for a black cat. But the nearest they came to getting one was a little boy who said his cat was going to have kittens pretty soon, and he would save a black one for them if there was a black one.

At the corner, they ran into Shorty Morton and Carol Jones, who were being followed by half a dozen cats. Striped cats, gray cats, yellow cats. But no black ones.

"Hey, what goes on here?" asked Billy.

"Oh, Shorty thinks he's so smart," said Carol. "He went right home and opened a can of sardines to catch a black cat with. Only he spilled sardine juice on his shoes and now we've got every cat in town following us."

Billy laughed so hard it made Shorty mad. "Go ahead, laugh," he said. "I don't notice *you've* got so many black cats."

"That's what you think," said Billy. "Come on, Peggy."

They went around the corner and up on a porch, and Billy rang the bell.

A little old lady answered the door. "We're on a scavenger hunt," explained Billy, "and we want to ask—"

"What? What?" she asked. "Speak up, I'm a little hard of hearing."

"A scavenger hunt!" Billy shouted. The old lady had never heard of a scavenger hunt before, and Billy had quite a time explaining what one was, but he finally got the idea across.

"How exciting!" she cried. "A 1924 penny. Why, I have a whole jar of pennies in the kitchen. Wait, I'll fetch it."

She brought the jar, and they helped her go through the pennies one at a time, reading the dates.

"1924!" shouted Billy, finally, holding up the penny. The old lady was almost as excited as he was, and asked eagerly, "Is there anything else you need?"

"No, thank you," said Billy, but Peggy said, "Yes, a black cat."

"A what?"

"A BLACK CAT!" shouted Peggy.

"Why, yes, I have one, but I don't know about lending it to you," she replied doubtfully. "You would have to take very good care of it, you know."

"Oh, we would, we would!" cried Peggy.

"And bring it right back," she added.

"Of course, right away," promised Peggy.

"Then wait a minute." She trotted off.

"But what'll I say to Fats, after all his trouble?" asked Billy.

"I don't care what you say to Fats," retorted Peggy.

They waited and waited, while Billy fidgeted, and finally the old lady returned carrying in both hands a black hat. It was an enormous hat, covered with ostrich feathers.

"Oh, thank you," gasped Peggy, "but I didn't say hat, I said—"

"You're welcome, my dear," replied the old lady. "But don't waste time thanking me. Run along and win your prize."

It took quite a while to explain, and when the old lady finally caught on, she said she was just as glad, because if anything happened to this hat she would never be able to find another.

Then Billy shoved the penny in his pocket with the sock and the pine cone, and grabbed the rake and lit out for Fats' house. Peggy followed with the Sunday paper, shouting, "Wait, wait!"

Billy ran up on Fats' porch and banged on the screen door. Bobby came to the door, eating a piece of bread and butter. "Where's Fats?" asked Billy breathlessly.

"Not here," mumbled Bobby.

"*What!*" exclaimed Billy.

"I told you so," said Peggy.

"But if you came for the black cat, I got it right in here. Fats said for me to give it to you," said Bobby, but he didn't unlock the screen.

"Well, give it to me," demanded Billy. "I'm in a hurry."

Bobby wasn't in any hurry. He took another bite and asked, "What'll you give me if I do?"

"I'll give you something if you don't!" shouted Billy. "You unlock this door and hand out that cat if you know what's good for you!"

"All right," said Bobby meekly. He got the cat and handed it out to Billy.

"Good old Fats," said Billy, stroking the cat. "I'll fill him up with ice cream if I have to bring it in a wheelbarrow. Come on, Peggy. You bring the rake."

They headed for Stew's house as fast as they could go. At the corner nearest the Wilsons', they overtook Gus Schultz and Sandra Riley. Gus was carrying a black cat with white feet. At least the cat was waltzing around on Gus' shoulders. Billy and Peggy didn't have any trouble passing *them*.

Then they saw two other couples approaching from the opposite direction. Their cats didn't look very black to Billy, but he wasn't taking any chances. He and Peggy put on a burst of speed, and just skimmed up the Wilsons' front steps ahead of the others.

Things were pretty crowded and brisk on the Wilsons' front porch for a few minutes. Mrs. Wilson was checking off the things the returning scavengers had brought, and all the cats were trying to start fights with all the other cats, and Billy was loudly pointing out that nobody else's cat was as black as his.

But finally Mrs. Wilson got things under control enough to announce that first everybody must take back the things they had borrowed, especially the cats. "Then hurry right back, and we'll have refreshments and give out the prizes," she said.

Several kids shouted, "Who won?"

Billy had his mouth open to say that he did, when he noticed Fats, standing quietly, in a far corner of the porch.

"Hey, what're *you* doing here?" he asked. "You weren't invited."

"He was, too," said Stew, stepping over beside Fats. "He's my partner, and we won the scavenger hunt."

"What!" shouted Billy.

"Sure," said Stew calmly, "I had everything but the cat, and I happened to go past Fats' house and he happened to have a black cat. So I invited him to be my partner."

"What black cat?" asked Billy suspiciously.

"They brought one, all right," Mrs. Wilson assured him. "But I believe they've already returned it."

"Sure, I hurried right back with it, and told Bobby not to give it to anybody but you," said Fats virtuously.

"Why, you—you—that was *my* cat you used," spluttered Billy.

"Well, you got it, didn't you?" asked Fats reasonably. "It was right there, waiting for you, wasn't it? Look, I'll even let you out of your part of the bargain. You don't have to bring me any refreshments."

"You bet I don't!" yelled Billy.

"Because as long as I'm here anyway, I'll just take care of my own refreshments," said Fats happily.

—MARION HOLLAND

Fats Wins a Prize

Along toward the end of school, there was a big drive to raise money to buy a movie projector, and whichever room raised the most money would win a prize.

"Look, we'll get a gang together and collect old newspapers," said Billy to Fats. "The junk yard's giving seventy cents a hundred."

"A hundred papers?" asked Fats.

"No, dopey—a hundred pounds."

"A hundred pounds!" exclaimed Fats. "Say, you got any idea how many papers it takes to make a hundred pounds?"

"Listen, the money's for a movie machine at school, isn't it?" demanded Billy.

"Yeah, but who gets to pick out the movies? The teachers, you bet. *Our Little Feathered Friends, Some Interesting Facts About Pig Iron.* Besides, it's too hot to work." Fats leaned back against a tree and yawned. "Go ahead, work yourself to death, but count me out."

"All right, all right. Just don't come around later, begging me to cut you in, that's all," said Billy angrily.

By the end of the week, everybody in Miss Dowd's room was turning in money except Fats, and Billy wasn't speaking to him any more. Then on Saturday, Fats heard his mother say, "I'd give anything if I just had a good excuse to get rid of all these awful old comic books. Look at them—all over the place."

It suddenly occurred to Fats that other mothers might feel the same way. So he got an old grocery carton and went right to work. He went from door to door, asking politely, "Do you have any old comic books that you could donate to raise money for a movie machine at our school?"

Well, it turned out that Fats was right. The mothers were simply tickled to death to clear out all the old limp comics that were cluttering up the house, and for such a good cause, too. Some places Fats got as many as twenty or thirty, and he had to make a lot of trips home to empty the carton, but it sure beat hauling loads of paper and scrap metal clear across town to the junk yard. He worked fast, because he had an idea that business would fall off as soon as all the kids started coming home to supper.

Monday after school he set up an old table on the sidewalk with a sign: *Bargains in Comics—Old but Still Good*. Then he dragged out a chair and settled back to read. The only trouble was that customers kept buying the comics before he had a chance to finish them.

They were mostly satisfied customers, too; but Billy came around, boiling mad, because his mother had handed Fats some of his favorite old comics, and he wanted them back. And he didn't see why he should have to pay for them, either.

But Fats reminded him that it was all for the sake of a movie machine at school. So then Billy said that by rights he ought to poke Fats one in the nose. But he didn't. He just walked off and hollered back that it would be a long time before he ever did Fats a favor again.

Well, when the money was all raised, it was Miss Dowd's room that had raised the most and won the prize. And the prize turned

99

out to be this: they were to see the very first movie, in their own room, and a lot of distinguished visitors were coming to see the movie, too—like members of the School Board and officers of the P.T.A.

Miss Dowd was in a perfect dither about it, and she started right in appointing committees to get ready for the big day. There was a Program Committee and a Decorations Committee and a Refreshments Committee, and even a Committee to Sandpaper and Varnish the Desk Tops. And an Aquarium Committee, because the goldfish tanks were so covered with green stuff you could hardly see the goldfish. Billy was chairman of this one.

Finally everybody in the room was on some committee or other except Fats. He figured Miss Dowd had forgotten about him, so he scrouged down in his seat and thought how lucky he was. But suddenly she called his name.

"Bruce Martin—stand up." Fats stood up and everybody looked at him and wondered what he had done now. He was wondering the same thing himself. "I know you will all be proud of Bruce when I tell you that he raised more money for our drive than any other single pupil in the school," announced Miss Dowd. "In recognition of his hard work and school spirit, I am appointing him to make the speech of welcome to our distinguished visitors."

"Speech?" croaked Fats. "What'll I *say?*"

But nobody heard him, because everybody started clapping, and it took Miss Dowd about ten minutes to get them to stop. After school, Fats asked Billy if he would help him with his speech, but Billy said coldly, "Huh, serves you right, selling other people's comics. Besides, after all that hard work and school spirit, writing a speech ought to be a cinch."

All the committees got to work right away, and what with holding meetings and taking trips to get supplies, they hardly showed up at school at all. Not even the Aquarium Committee, though Fats couldn't see how cleaning out a few fish tanks was so much of a job.

But somehow Billy persuaded Miss Dowd that the goldfish were looking mighty poorly. The whole Aquarium Committee had to go to the library to do research on the Care and Feeding of Goldfish, and they didn't come back until three o'clock. Then they polished up the tanks and put in fresh sand and water plants, and threw out all the fish food, because they had read in some book that fish do better on live food. So they had to go out every morning with jars and scoop up pond water with little wiggly things in it for the goldfish to eat.

Only Fats stayed right at his desk, sweating over a speech of welcome for distinguished visitors, except when he had to move to somebody else's desk to let the sandpapering and varnishing committee work on his. He used up three pencils, chewing them down at one end and sharpening them at the other, before he got a speech to suit Miss Dowd.

And then he still had to learn it by heart and practice saying it with gestures. He did this at home, in his own room with the door locked, until he discovered that his kid brothers were outside looking through the keyhole. So then he quit practicing and just hoped he would break a leg or the school would burn down.

But the big day arrived, and he hadn't broken a leg, and the school hadn't burned down. And even though it was the hottest day of the year, his mother made him wear a necktie and his new suit, coat and all. When he got to school, he went around behind the lockers and began mumbling to himself, "Fellow classmates and honored guests, on behalf of Miss Dowd's room, I—uh—" He dug into his pants pocket, where he had been carrying his speech around for a week. But he was wearing his new pants. The pocket was empty.

Fats felt hot all over, but his hands were cold. "Fellow classmates," he whispered again.

Then the bell rang, and he had to take his seat. In a blur he watched the distinguished guests come in and seat themselves. And then Miss Dowd called out his name.

Fats stumbled up the aisle and cleared his throat. "Fellow classmates—" The words came out in a small squeak. He tried again. "Fellow classmates," he bellowed. He couldn't think of what came next, and his right ankle itched something fierce, and he didn't dare scratch. He looked desperately at Miss Dowd.

"Why, Miss Dowd," he blurted out. "There's a great big mosquito on your cheek. Slap it, quick!"

Miss Dowd slapped, but not quickly enough. Suddenly the whole room seemed to be full of mosquitoes.

The lady president of the P.T.A. stood up, fanning at the air around her head. "I can't stand mosquitoes!" she exclaimed.

"Fellow classmates and honored guests—" said Fats. But all the fellow classmates and honored guests were swatting mosquitoes. Shorty Morton swatted one on Gus Schultz so hard that Gus sat right down in the aisle.

"—on behalf of Miss Dowd's room—" Fats went on, but his voice was droned out by Miss Dowd's voice.

"Year after year," said Miss Dowd, looking straight at the Chairman of the School Board, "I have requested that these windows be screened, and now—"

Fats gave up and went down to the basement and got the janitor, and then he went quietly back to his own seat and sat down. By the time the janitor had sprayed all the mosquitoes and aired out the room, Miss Dowd was so confused and upset that she forgot all about Fats' speech of welcome, and just signaled to the man at the movie machine to go ahead. After the movie, the Refreshment Committee took over, and that was one committee that really made sense to Fats. He loosened his belt and his necktie and pitched in.

As the class filed out at noon, Billy grabbed Fats by the sleeve. "Stick around a couple of minutes, will you?" he asked. "I could use a little help with the fish."

"Are you crazy or something?" demanded Fats. "I'm not on your old committee."

"I know, but—look, you know where all those mosquitoes came from?"

"Sure. In the windows," replied Fats.

"Yeah, that's what I thought at first. But you know what I been feeding these goldfish?"

"What?"

"Mosquito larvae, that's what," said Billy. "That's what the books said to feed 'em. Only the books didn't say how many they'd eat, and I guess maybe I got ahead of 'em. Then it's been so hot the last few days—well, they just up and hatched out, that's all."

Fats took it in slowly. "You mean you hatched out all those mosquitoes right here, right in this room?"

"Yep."

"Oh boy, wait'll Miss Dowd finds out. Will you ever be in trouble!"

"She isn't going to find out," said Billy calmly. "We'll just dump out all this water and put in fresh, and there won't be any more mosquitoes."

"Where do you get that 'we' stuff?" demanded Fats. "You're the guy that wouldn't even help me with my speech, remember?"

"Help you!" exclaimed Billy. "You didn't have to make your old speech, did you? And on account of why? On account of *my* mosquitoes, that's why!"

Fats thought this over. "You talked me into it," he said finally. "And look—you know your comics? Well, I sort of kept track of who bought them. You come on home with me, after, and we'll get some of the comics I had left over. Then we'll go around to the kids' houses that bought yours and trade 'em back. O.K.?"

"O.K.," said Billy.

—MARION HOLLAND

Santa Claus Knows

It was the week before Christmas holidays, and it seemed to Billy that school would never end. He sat and scowled at the paper on his desk. So far, all it said was:

William Kidwell *December 15*

Christmas Customs of Other Lands

This was Miss Dowd's idea of something to write about, not Billy's. He stared at the ceiling, and wished there would be a fire drill, or, better still, a real fire.

A little girl from second grade scuttled in and laid a note on Miss Dowd's desk and scuttled out again. Miss Dowd read the note and said, "Bruce Martin." Billy never really got used to hearing Fats called Bruce. Neither did Fats. He jumped and then went up to the desk. Miss Dowd said something to him in a low voice. Fats got red in the face and went back to his seat and pretended to be writing very hard.

Billy couldn't hear what Miss Dowd said, but Jack Berger, in the front seat, heard, so pretty soon everybody in the room knew.

Fats was to report to the principal's office right after school. Everybody stared hard at Fats, but he pretended not to notice. He looked plenty worried, though, and Billy did a little worrying, too, on his own account. His trouble was that he couldn't think of a single thing that Miss Griswold, the principal, could want to see Fats about that she wouldn't want to see him about, too.

When the bell rang, Fats walked right down the hall to Miss Griswold's office. Billy and a couple of other fellows hung around outside, but they couldn't hear a thing. Then Miss Lovejoy, the kindergarten teacher, came along and walked into the office, too. One of Fats' kid brothers was in kindergarten, so Billy began to hope that all this was something about Bobby, and not about Fats, after all.

The other fellows lost interest and went away, but Billy noticed that Miss Lovejoy hadn't quite closed the door. He accidentally leaned against it a little, and the first thing he knew, he was in the office, too. Miss Griswold was smiling at Fats, so Billy stayed.

"You know the Christmas entertainment is to be Thursday afternoon, in the auditorium," she was saying to Fats. Well, Billy and Fats knew that, all right. "But the kindergarten children go home at noon, so Miss Lovejoy is planning a special party in the morning, just for them. Now, one of the parents has given the school this perfectly beautiful—Here it is."

She reached into a big box and pulled out a Santa Claus suit and held it up. It was bright red, with real fur trimmings, and Billy could see that there was a cap and whiskers, and even shiny boots, to go with it.

"Isn't it lovely?" she said to Fats. "The minute I saw it, I thought of you. I'm sure it will fit perfectly." She held it up against him, and he started backing away, but when he backed as far as the wall, he had to stop. "There now," she said to Miss Lovejoy. "Won't he make a perfectly splendid Santa for your party?"

"Oh boy," said Billy. "He won't even need any stuffings."
Fats gave him a dirty look.

"You won't have to do much," Miss Lovejoy explained to Fats.
"Just hand out the candy and presents. I'll have everything all
ready. And these little verses I have written won't take you
long to memorize, I'm sure."

She held out a sheet of paper, but Fats put his hands behind
his back.

"No thanks," he mumbled. "I wouldn't be any good at it,
honest I wouldn't. Anyway, I wouldn't fool those kindergarten
kids for a minute. My kid brother is in kindergarten, and those
kids are all over our house half the time. They all know me,
honest they do." He looked desperately at Billy. "You tell them,"
he said. "I wouldn't be any good at it, would I?"

"Sure you would," said Billy soothingly. He took the paper

from Miss Lovejoy. "He can learn this all right. I'll help him with it. He'll be fine, don't worry."

"Of course he will," beamed Miss Lovejoy.

"Sure, sure," said Billy, getting Fats by the arm and steering him toward the door. "Well, we better go now, and get right to work on this."

"A fine friend you turned out to be," said Fats bitterly, when they were outside. "Hey! Where are you going now?"

"Down to the auditorium. That's where the party is going to be." The stage was on a low platform at one end of the auditorium, and it was already set up for a play one of the upper grades was going to give. There was a big fireplace made out of cardboard, with an imitation red paper fire in it.

Billy looked it over. "The kids in the kindergarten will expect Santa to come down the chimney," he said. "So I guess you better come down the chimney."

"I don't care what they expect!" roared Fats. "I won't do it! Anyway, there isn't any chimney."

"Not now there isn't, but we can fix one," said Billy thoughtfully. He shoved Miss Lovejoy's verses at Fats. "Get to work on this. I got to catch Miss Griswold before she goes."

Fats was muttering gloomily to himself, "Ho-ho, little kiddies, ho-ho!"

Billy was back in five minutes, waving a paper. "What's that?" asked Fats suspiciously. "More verses?"

"It's an excuse from Miss Griswold for both of us to get out of school all day tomorrow, that's what."

Fats cheered up a little. "No fooling? But what for? The party isn't till day after tomorrow."

"Why, we got work to do," said Billy virtuously. "Tomorrow

morning we fix the fireplace so it looks like you're coming down the chimney, and tomorrow afternoon we rehearse. Miss Griswold is tickled to death to see us taking a real interest in giving the kindergarten a good time."

"Where do you get this *we* stuff?" asked Fats. "I do all the work, and you get out of school."

Miss Dowd didn't act very pleased the next morning when they walked in and showed her the note from the principal, but there wasn't anything she could do about it. Everybody in the room was dying of curiosity, but there wasn't anything they could do about it, either. Billy and Fats just stuck their noses up in the air, and marched out the door.

It was pretty easy, fixing the fireplace on the stage with some black curtains and a ladder they borrowed from the janitor. The hardest part was making it take all morning.

After lunch, Miss Griswold came down to rehearse Fats. At first, she wanted him to come down the chimney with his pack on his back, but the cardboard fireplace turned out to be a tight fit, just for Fats. So they tried having Billy drop the bag down after him, and it worked fine.

Then she rehearsed Fats on the verses. By the time she let him quit, he was pretty tired of saying them, and Billy was pretty tired of listening to them. But Miss Lovejoy seemed to enjoy every minute of it, probably because she was the one who wrote the verses.

Even so, the rehearsal was over by two o'clock. "Now what?" asked Fats, when he and Billy were alone. "*Christmas Customs of Other Lands?*"

"That fireplace is sort of wobbly still," said Billy, wobbling the fireplace a little. "I guess it could use some more fixing!"

111

So they got a couple of hammers, and every time anybody looked into the auditorium they did a little hammering until the three o'clock bell rang.

Next morning, Billy called for Fats about eight o'clock. Fats said he didn't feel so good this morning, and maybe he should stay home from school today. Billy just waited around while Fats ate breakfast, and then he said to Fats' mother that he didn't think that anybody that ate a dish of cereal with two bananas and five pieces of buttered toast and two fried eggs was sick enough to stay home from school. Fats' mother agreed with him.

Billy got the costume from Miss Griswold's office and borrowed a jar of rubber cement and a piece of chalk. Then he got Fats dressed in a little room behind the stage where there was a light and a mirror. Fats kept squirming around and saying, "Do I have to wear all this stuff? I feel like such a dope."

Everything fitted fine, even the whiskers. There was a string to tie them on with, but Billy stuck them on with rubber cement besides, so they wouldn't flop around.

"Ow!" yelled Fats. "That itches."

"Shut up and stand still," said Billy unsympathetically. "Do you want this stuff in your eyes?" He rubbed some red chalk on Fats' nose and on his cheeks above the whiskers. Then he backed up and looked him over.

"Golly!" he exclaimed. "You don't have to worry about the kindergarten kids recognizing you. Here, take a look!"

Fats edged up to the mirror and sneaked a look in it. Then he took a good, long look. He settled his belt and stuck out his chest and stomach. "Not bad, not bad," he admitted.

"You don't even sound like yourself," said Billy.

112

"That's because every time I open my mouth, I get it full of whiskers," growled Fats, but he wasn't really complaining. In fact, Billy could hardly drag him away from the mirror, in time to come down the ladder behind the fireplace when the kindergarten got through singing "Jingle Bells."

There was one bad moment when Fats was squeezing out through the fireplace opening. The fireplace began to sway back and forth, and if Billy hadn't hung onto it from behind, the whole thing would have fallen down flat. Then Billy dropped the bag of presents down, and Fats reached in and got it.

A little girl squealed, "Ooo, look! *Santa Claus!*" and Fats started right in "Ho-hoing."

Billy sneaked out the back way, and around by the corridor and into the back of the auditorium.

Fats was just finishing up the verses, and they were certainly going over big with the kindergarten. The kids were all sitting on the edges of their chairs, with their eyes and mouths wide open, all except one little boy in the back row. He was poking the little boys next to him and pulling the hair of the little girl in front of him. Miss Lovejoy, who was sitting over at one side, kept looking at him and shaking her head, but Billy could have told her that *that* wasn't going to do much good.

Fats started fishing presents out of the bag and calling out names. One little girl thought she was supposed to tell him what she wanted for Christmas. "And don't forget the doll with open-and-shut eyes, that drinks water out of a bottle and wets its pants," she said in a high, shrill voice.

"Have you been a good little girl?" Fats asked solemnly. "Been minding your mother and eating all your crusts?"

The little girl nodded her head.

"Fine, fine," said Fats. "I'll remember that."

The little boy in the back row was still making a big nuisance of himself. Fats groped around in the bag for a minute and pulled out a present. He called, "Johnny Walters!"

The little boy in the back row walked up to the stage. He stuck

his hands in his pockets, and said in a loud voice, "Aw, you're just a fake. There's no such thing as Santa Claus."

"There is, too," shouted several kids.

"There is not!" yelled Johnny. "How could any old Santa Claus tell if you've been good or bad, way up at the North Pole?" He grabbed the present, and started back toward his seat.

"*Johnny Walters!*" said Fats, in an awful voice. "You come right back here."

Johnny stopped in his tracks. All the other kids got very quiet.

Fats pointed his finger at Johnny. "So you think Santa Claus doesn't know whether you've been good or bad?"

"No, he doesn't," said Johnny. "How could he?"

"Santa Claus knows plenty," said Fats in a deep voice. "Santa Claus knows plenty about *you*, Johnny Walters. He knows all

about the time you took the wheels off your sister's doll carriage to put on a scooter. He knows all about the time when you poured ink in a goldfish bowl. He knows all about the time you let the air out of the Rickers' tires. He even knows who broke the window in the Caseys' garage. You thought nobody knew that, didn't you? Well, let me tell you, *Santa Claus knows.* You want to hear some more of the things Santa Claus knows?"

"No," said Johnny in a small voice.

"He knows what you want the most for Christmas, too. Well, he hasn't made up his mind yet. It all depends on how you act between now and Christmas. Now you can go back to your seat and think that over."

After that, everything went as smooth as pie. Billy could hardly keep from laughing out loud when Bobby Martin, Fats' own little brother, went up to get his present. Fats mentioned that Santa Claus would be pleased if Bobby never went into his big brother's room and messed up his things any more. Bobby promised, solemnly and respectfully.

Billy just got around behind the stage in time to help Fats climb back up the chimney. "Wow! You were swell!" exclaimed Billy. "Was all that stuff true about Johnny?"

"True? It was *my* fish bowl he poured the ink into! Say, I did all right, didn't I?"

Just then Miss Griswold came up onto the stage. "I was watching, from near the door," she said. "And I just had to come around and tell you what a splendid performance you gave!" She shook hands, first with Fats, then with Billy. "I want to thank both of you on behalf of Miss Lovejoy and the kindergarten children."

As she left, the principal added, "I'll stop by your room and tell Miss Dowd that you'll be back as soon as you get out of costume."

Fats took one last look at himself in the mirror. "You know, I sort of hate to take this stuff off."

"Yeah, and it's only about ten-thirty," said Billy. "And, oh brother, is Miss Dowd ever going to put us to work!"

Fats groaned. "I don't suppose Miss Dowd would believe it, if we walked in at noon and said it took an hour and a half to take off the Santa suit."

"Say, it might at that," said Billy thoughtfully. "Do you know anything that will dissolve rubber cement?"

Fats felt his whiskers. "No, don't you?" he asked in alarm.

"No," admitted Billy. "When I was sticking them on, I never thought about taking them off."

"Well, start thinking about it now!" roared Fats.

"Keep your shirt on, keep your shirt on," said Billy. "If we can't do it any other way, we can always peel them off a little at a time. It ought not to take more than an hour and a half."

—FROM *Billy Had a System* BY MARION HOLLAND

Zip and the Alarming Clock

Now I've heard tell there was a man named Foolish Tom who was the most foolish man in the world. But he had an old brown hound dog named Zip who was plenty smart.

One day Tom went fishing. He sat down on the creek bank under a sycamore tree, and dropped his line in the water. It wasn't long till he heard somebody coming across the field.

Tom could see a fishing pole sticking up through the bushes. "Howdy," he called out.

"Howdy," answered the fishing pole.

"Come and set a spell," said Tom.

"Don't mind if I do," answered the fishing pole, coming around a little willow tree, and there stood Reuben Hill. He came over and sat down.

"Are you feeling fine, Tom?" asked Reuben, dropping his line in the water.

"Tolerable," answered Tom.

"Looks like rain."

"Dog, if it don't," said Tom.

"How's Zip?" asked Reuben.

"Smart as ever," answered Tom. "I don't reckon there's another dog in this wide world that's got more natural-born brains than Zip."

"Well, now, that might be," Reuben nodded slowly, "and then again it might not."

Tom pulled his line up out of the water so fast he gave an old yellow catfish indigestion.

"Reuben Hill!" Tom looked mad. "You ain't trying to tell me you think your hound, Old Blue, is as smart as Zip! Why, you know Zip can read and write!"

"Well, shucks, Foolish Tom, all them little bitty children over at the schoolhouse can do that, can't they?"

Tom looked as thoughtful as he could. "I reckon they can, Reuben," he answered. Directly he scratched his head and said, "But Zip can chop wood and milk the cow."

"Why, Foolish Tom, I reckon everybody hereabouts can do that," said Reuben.

Tom looked very down-in-the-mouth. "I reckon they can, Reuben," he finally answered. He studied for a spell and then he said, "But Zip can catch a heap of rabbits!"

Reuben laughed out loud and slapped his knee. "Now, Tom, if that don't take the rag off the bush! Why, once I had an old blind hound dog that could catch rabbits."

Tom scratched his head again. "I reckon you're right, Reuben," he said. "Zip might not be so smart after all."

"Tom," said Reuben with a sly smile, "I'll tell you what my hound, Old Blue, can do, and if you don't think he's smarter than Zip, I'll give you all the melons in my watermelon patch. But if you think Blue's the smartest dog you ever heard tell of, you must give me that new alarming clock Zip fetched from town the other day."

So Tom said that would be fine. He did love watermelons.

"Well, now, my Old Blue," began Reuben, "when we go possum hunting, Old Blue runs along and when he comes to a tree with a big possum in it, he props a big stick up against the tree. And when he comes to a tree with a little possum in it, he leans a little old stick up against the tree. Then all I have to do is come along and take my choice. Now can Zip do that?"

Tom shook his head sadly. "Naw, Zip can't do that. He has to climb up the tree after them possums." He picked up his fishing pole. "Come on, Reuben, and I'll get you that alarming clock. I got to be fair. Blue is smarter than Zip."

After Reuben had left with the clock, Tom sat on the porch and thought about that watermelon patch. He did love watermelon. Along about the middle of August, he was going to miss those melons a-cooling in the spring. Of course, Zip was going to miss that alarming clock, too.

That clock was a heap of help when it came to milking the cows on time. Zip had been mighty proud of that clock. In fact, the more Tom thought about Zip and that clock, the more uneasy he began to feel.

Along toward sundown, Tom saw Zip coming up from the fields, and something told him he'd been a mite hasty about letting Reuben have that alarming clock. After all it belonged to Zip.

He got down off the porch and ran and squatted down in the weeds by the house.

Zip came up to the house and leaned his hoe against the porch. He went in the house, and directly came out again.

"Tom," he hollered. "Foolish Tom!"

But Foolish Tom didn't say a word.

Zip looked all around and saw Tom's old black hat sticking up out of the weeds.

"What's that over in the weeds?" wondered Zip out loud.

Foolish Tom put his hands over his eyes. He was so foolish,

he thought if he couldn't see Zip, then Zip couldn't see him. Then Tom began to cackle like a hen that's laid an egg.

Zip walked over and watched Tom sitting in the weeds, cackling.

"Well, now," remarked Zip, "here's that old hen that always lays in the weeds. I'll just wring her neck now and be done with it."

Tom took his hands down from his eyes quick and said, "Oh, please don't wring my neck, Zip. It's just me."

"Foolish Tom," said Zip in a stern voice, "where is my new alarming clock?"

And then Foolish Tom had to tell how he'd made the bet with Reuben Hill and lost the bet, and how Reuben Hill got the clock.

Zip shook his head. "Tom, you are so foolish that I ought to put you out to pasture with Sheriff Brown's donkey. Better'n that, maybe I can still get even with Reuben Hill."

That night, just as the moon rose, Zip walked over the top of a hill and met Reuben coming up the other side. Reuben had a sack slung over his shoulder, and Old Blue trotted behind him.

"Evening, Reuben," said Zip.

"Howdy, Zip," answered Reuben. He looked kind of uneasy.

Zip put on his manners. "Reuben, if you don't mind, I'd like to watch you and Blue hunt this evening."

"Why sure, Zip," Reuben answered with a little laugh. "We're glad to have you."

Reuben and Zip walked through the woods together, and Old Blue ran on ahead sniffing and snuffing.

By and by Reuben showed Zip a little stick leaning against a tree. "See here," he said, "this means there's a possum in this tree."

"Do tell," said Zip politely.

"Yes," said Reuben, "but it's just a little bitty possum. I don't aim to fool with little ones."

They walked on till they came to another tree with a stick leaning against it. This time it was a big stick.

"Now, you just watch, Zip, whilst I shinny up this tree. I'll come back with a sure enough real big feller," Reuben said. Sure enough, when he came down, he had a big fat possum in his poke.

"Well, Reuben," said Zip, "if you're after big fellers, you missed the biggest one. Look over yonder."

Zip pointed to a tree with a great big stick propped against it.

"Whoopee!" yelled Reuben. "That must be a whopper!" And he ran to the tree and began to climb up it.

In a minute a most terrifying uproar came from up in the tree. Such a squalling and hollering and roaring you never heard.

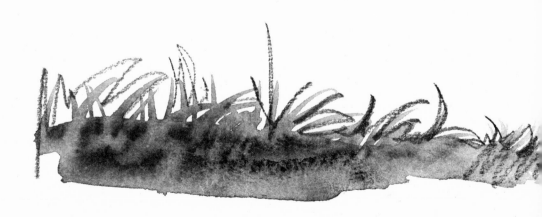

And then Reuben came crashing down out of the tree with a big wildcat right behind him, spitting and clawing for dear life.

"Help me, Zip! Help!" he screamed.

So Zip ran at the wildcat and chased him off into the bushes. Then he helped Reuben up and they set off for home.

When they got to Reuben's house, Zip helped him into a rocking chair and fetched him some turpentine to put on the scratches.

Reuben groaned. "I never heard tell of such a dumb hound dog!"

"It's a crying shame," said Zip. "I'd of thought Old Blue would have been able to tell a possum from a wildcat."

Reuben moaned and groaned again, easing himself down on his pillows.

"You know, Reuben," said Zip, "it's a funny thing. I had a new alarming clock just like that one you got upon the shelf. And it just disappeared, clean as a wink!"

"Take mine, Zip," groaned Reuben, holding his head. "You're welcome to it."

Zip took the clock down off the shelf and got ready to go home. "I thought I'd drop by your melon patch and take home a couple of melons," Zip said.

"Help yourself, Zip," said Reuben. "Anytime you like."

Zip went on out to Reuben's melon patch. It was bright moonlight. Zip chuckled as he looked around at all the melons in Reuben's patch. He thumped a few, and when he found two that seemed the ripest, he took off down the road toward his house.

He stopped by the spring and put one melon down in the water to cool. He took the other one on up to the house.

By and by Zip and Foolish Tom sat on the porch, eating watermelon and throwing rinds in the yard.

Zip spit some seeds out into the darkness and he began to chuckle. "I found that tree with the wildcat in it quick enough," he told Tom. "But I about thought I wasn't ever going to find a stick big enough to lean up against it."

Foolish Tom was surprised. "Do you mean to say, Zip," he asked, "that it was you who put that stick up against the tree with the wildcat in it?"

Zip laughed. "I'll tell you what," he told Tom, "I may be dumber than Old Blue, but I'm smarter than Reuben Hill any day in the week!"

—WILLIAM O. STEELE

The Glorious Whitewasher

Saturday morning was come, and all the summer world was bright and brimming with life. There was a song in every heart. Cardiff Hill, beyond the village, was green, dreamy, inviting.

Tom appeared on the sidewalk before Aunt Polly's house with a bucket of whitewash and a long-handled brush. He surveyed the fence, and all gladness left him and a deep melancholy settled down upon his spirit. Thirty yards of board fence nine feet high. Sighing, he dipped his brush and passed it along the topmost plank; repeated the operation; did it again; compared the insignificant whitewashed streak with the far-reaching continent of unwhitewashed fence, and sat down on a tree-box discouraged.

Jim came skipping along with a tin pail, singing, on his way to get water from the pump. Getting water from the pump always had been hateful work in Tom's eyes, but now it did not strike him so. There was company at the pump—girls and boys having a good time and in no hurry to carry the water home. So Tom, by giving Jim one of his best marbles, was able to persuade Jim to whitewash for him while he went for water. But just then Aunt Polly appeared and sent Jim flying down the street with his pail while Tom whitewashed with vigor.

But Tom's energy did not last. He thought of the fun he had planned for this day, and his sorrows multiplied. Soon the free boys would come along on all sorts of delicious expeditions, and make fun of Tom for having to work. He got out his worldly

wealth—bits of toys, marbles and trash; enough to buy an ex-
change of *work* but not half enough to buy so much as half an
hour of pure freedom. He returned the things to his pocket and
gave up the idea of trying to buy the boys. At this dark moment
a magnificent inspiration burst upon him!

He took up his brush and went tranquilly to work. Ben Rogers hove in sight—the very boy, of all boys, whose ridicule Tom had been dreading. Ben was eating an apple and giving a long, melodious whoop at intervals, followed by a deep-toned ding-dong-dong, for he was personating a steamboat. He was boat and captain and engine-bells combined, so he imagined himself standing on the hurricane-deck giving orders and executing them. He kept shouting orders to his imaginary crew and trying gauge-cocks and ringing bells.

Tom went on whitewashing—paid no attention to the steamboat. Ben stared a moment and then said: "Hi-yi! *You're* up a stump, ain't you!"

No answer. Tom surveyed his last touch with the eye of an artist, then he gave his brush another gentle sweep and surveyed the result, as before. Ben ranged up alongside of him. Tom's mouth watered for the apple, but he stuck to his work.

Ben said: "Hello, old chap, you got to work, hey?"

Tom wheeled suddenly and said: "Why, it's you, Ben! I warn't noticing."

"Say—I'm going in a-swimming, I am. Don't you wish you could? But of course you'd druther *work*—wouldn't you? 'Course you would!"

Tom contemplated the boy a bit, and said: "What do you call work?"

"Why, ain't *that* work?"

Tom resumed his whitewashing and answered carelessly: "Well, maybe it is, and maybe it ain't. All I know is, it suits Tom Sawyer."

"Oh come now, you don't mean to let on that you *like* it?"

The brush continued to move.

"Like it? Well, I don't see why I oughtn't to like it. Does a boy get a chance to whitewash a fence every day?"

That put the thing in a new light. Ben stopped nibbling his apple. Tom swept his brush daintily back and forth—stepped back to note the effect—added a touch here and there—criticized the effect again—Ben watching every move and getting more and more interested, more and more absorbed. Presently he said: "Say, Tom, let me whitewash a little."

Tom considered, was about to consent; but he altered his mind.

"No—no—I reckon it wouldn't hardly do, Ben. You see, Aunt Polly's awful particular about this fence—right here on the street, you know—but if it was the back fence I wouldn't mind and *she* wouldn't. Yes, she's awful particular about this fence; it's got to be done very careful; I reckon there ain't one boy in a thousand, maybe two thousand, that can do it the way it's got to be done."

"No—is that so? Oh, come, now—lemme just try. Only just a little—I'd let you, if you was me, Tom."

"Ben, I'd like to, honest injun; but Aunt Polly—well, Jim wanted to do it, but she wouldn't let him; Sid wanted to do it, and she wouldn't let Sid. Now don't you see how I'm fixed? If you was to tackle this fence and anything was to happen to it—"

"Oh, shucks, I'll be just as careful. Now lemme try. Say—I'll give you the core of my apple."

"Well, here—No, Ben, now don't. I'm afeared—"

"I'll give you *all* of it!"

Tom gave up the brush with reluctance in his face, but alacrity in his heart. And while the late steamer *Big Missouri* worked and sweated in the sun, the retired artist sat on a barrel in the shade close by, dangled his legs, munched his apple, and planned

129

the slaughter of more innocents. There was no lack of material; boys happened along every little while; they came to jeer, but remained to whitewash. By the time Ben was fagged out, Tom had traded the next chance to Billy Fisher for a kite, in good repair; and when *he* played out, Johnny Miller bought in for a dead rat and a string to swing it with—and so on, and so on, hour after hour. And when the middle of the afternoon came, from being a poor poverty-stricken boy in the morning, Tom

was literally rolling in wealth. He had beside the things before mentioned, twelve marbles, part of a jew's-harp, a piece of blue bottle-glass to look through, a spool cannon, a key that wouldn't unlock anything, a fragment of chalk, a glass stopper of a decanter, a tin soldier, a couple of tadpoles, six firecrackers, a kitten, a brass door-knob, a dog-collar—but no dog—the handle of a knife, four pieces of orange-peel, and a dilapidated old window-sash.

He had had a nice, good, idle time all the while—plenty of company—and the fence had three coats of whitewash on it! If he hadn't run out of whitewash, he would have bankrupted every boy in the village.

Tom said to himself that it was not such a hollow world, after all. He had discovered a great law of human action, without knowing it—namely, that in order to make a man or boy covet a thing, it is only necessary to make the thing difficult to attain.

The boy mused awhile over the substantial change which had taken place in his worldly circumstances, and then wended toward headquarters to report.

—ADAPTED BY MILDRED CORELL LUCKHARDT
FROM *The Adventures of Tom Sawyer*
BY MARK TWAIN

The Lass That Couldn't Be Frighted

There once was a lass and naught could ever give her a fright! At least, that was what folks said about her.

She lived all alone on a bit of a farm that stood in the forest. Her mother died when she was a wee thing, and her father—the poor man—was never much use to her, he being more often found at the inn, in the village nearby, than at home or at work. Besides that, one day he just wandered away somewhere, and wherever it was he went he never came back.

When it was plain that he was gone for good, folks told her she'd best come down to live in the village, seeing she had no kin of her own to take her in.

"But why should I?" she asked. "I'm very well as I am."

"Lawks!" said the folks. "And are you not afraid to bide by yourself in that lonesome place? 'Tis enough to fright the soul out of a body!"

"Think of all the wild beasts!" they said.

"Hoots!" said she. "Well you know there are no wild beasts in the forest, barring a hart, or happen a hare after the kail, or a wee fox trying for the hen run."

But the cottagers were awful uneasy about her. For you never could tell! The forest was big and dark. Anything could be in it—and there might be worse things abroad by night than wild beasties.

"What then?" she asked.

They looked to the left and they looked to the right, and then they put their heads close to hers and whispered, "*The Wee People.*"

"Och!" laughed she. "Goblins and ghaisties and such like! Goodwife's tales to scare the bairns with!"

They were horrified at that. Did she not believe in the Wee Folks? Well, she wouldn't say "aye," nor would she say "nay" to that. But what she did say was, that if there were any of them, why she didn't mind them at all.

So they gave up talking to her about it, but what they said to each other was that she was uncommon brave for a lassie. And that's how the story came about that she was a lassie that couldn't be frighted.

The strange thing was that it was true. With her dog and her cat she was well able to keep the hares from her garden and the foxes from her hens. And if a bear had come to rob her hives (though, of course, there were no bears in the forest) she'd just have twisted his ear and spatted him back to the forest with the flat of her hand to his backside. As for the fairies—well, if there were any about let them keep to their ways and she'd keep to hers.

With her house and her garden and her cow and her two sheep and her hens and her beehives she was well fixed, and with her dog and her cat for company what more could she ask?

True, she seldom saw money from one year's end to the other, but the things from her wee farm that she had over what she needed for her own use she could trade in at the shop in the village for whatever she couldn't raise or make for herself. So what good was money to her, the way things were? And being contented, she was as happy as the day is long.

Then one day one of the lads from the village looked at her and saw that she was the bonniest lass in all the countryside. Then, having taken one look he took another, and saw that she had come to an age when she might well think of getting married. He went and told a friend or two and those took the word of it to one or two more, and in no time all the lads for miles around were clustered at her gate like bees in a swarm, all buzzing around at her to make her pick one of them to wed. All the lads but one, that is, and that one was Wully the weaver's son, who had a croft on the hillside over against the forest. When one of the lads told him she was awful bonny he said, aye he'd known that for long. And when they said she was old enough to wed he said that he knew that, too. And when they asked if he wasn't going to be wooing her the lads all thought he was plain daft, for he said, nay he thought he'd just bide his time, and up he climbed to his croft and tended his sheep.

Little good came to the ones who stayed to woo her, for she wouldn't have any of them.

"Why should I?" she asked them.

To protect her? Well, she hadn't had trouble doing that for herself. Besides, she had her dog.

For money? Well, that she didn't want nor need.

For love? And she only laughed, and said that when the lad she could fancy came along she'd give that her consideration. But, for the present, she'd stay as she was.

So at last all the lads were so discouraged that they left her, to look elsewhere, which did not displease her at all.

The lads who had given up trying to win her told Wully the weaver's son that maybe he'd done well not to waste his time on such a headstrong lassie, and besides it wasn't natural for a lass not to be afraid of aught. But all Wully said was, "Och, we'll see then," and went on tending his sheep.

So days went by and weeks went by, and then one evening the lassie went to the meal bin to fetch herself some meal to make her some bannocks for supper.

"There now!" she said. "When I fill the bowl the bin will be empty!" and she scraped at the bottom of the bin. "There'll be no oatmeal for the porridge in the morn," said she.

So she made up her mind that as soon as she'd had her supper she'd take a sack of meal to have it ground at Hughie the miller's mill.

When she'd baked her bannocks and eaten them she went to the shed and filled a sack with oats, and taking it on her arm off she set for the mill. 'Twas a fine warm night, so she enjoyed the walk, but when she got to the mill the house beside it was dark and the mill shut tight, for the miller and all his family had gone off somewhere for a visit and there was nobody at home to grind her oats for her.

She set her sack on the sill of the house and sat herself down beside of it, to consider what she was to do.

Lachie, the miller, had a mill, too, but it lay over on the edge of the next village, a long ways off. It would be far to go, but she could think of nothing better to do if she was going to have porridge in the morning.

When she left Hughie's mill, dusk was closing in, and when she got to Lachie's mill the night was as dark as the inside of one of the caves of Cruachan. Lachie's mill was idle and still and the door was locked, but that did not trouble her, for the house of the miller, over the way, showed a light. So she went up to the house and clackit at the door.

The miller came to the door and stood there staring at her.

"I've brought you a bag of oats to be ground at the mill," said the lass. And when the miller said nothing she added civilly, " 'Tis sorry I am to trouble you so late, but I've no meal in the house at all against the morn."

"I'll grind no meal in the mill tonight," said the miller then. "Come back on the tomorrow's morn."

But the lass wasn't going to be put off that way. "I'm telling you I've no meal in the house for the morning's porridge!" she said impatiently.

"Come back fasting then," said the miller, "for I'll grind no meal tonight!"

"Well then, give me the key to the mill," the lass told him, "and I'll grind my meal myself."

"Woman!" roared the miller, "I will not grind your meal nor will I give you the key! For when anyone grinds grain in the mill o' nights a great ugly goblin comes up through the floor and steals the grain and beats him black and blue!"

"Hoots! Toots! to your goblin!" the lass shouted back at him. "I'll grind my grain, goblin or no goblin! *Miller, give me the key!*"

So determined was she that the miller fetched the key, but he would not give it to her until he had called his wife and all in his house to witness that he was not to blame whatever happened to her.

Then she took the key, and the miller's wife lit a lanthorn and gave it to her, to light her so that she could see to grind her meal.

The lass went off to the mill and unlocked the door. She opened it and looked all about, but there was nothing there. So she went and opened the water into the race, and the mill wheel began to turn around. Clack! Clack! Whish! Clack! Clack! Whish! Clack! Clack! Whish! went the mill wheel.

So then she poured the grain into the hopper and sat herself down to rest a minute while the grain went through, for the long walk had tired her a little and she still had to walk back. But it was not long till the meal was through, so she let it pour out into her sack. When all her meal was in the sack she knotted the top, and she said to herself said she, "Well! There's nothing here to fash myself about!"

And just then up through the floor rose a great ugly goblin! He had a big black club in one hand and he stretched the other one out to grab her sack of meal!

"No you don't!" shrieked the lass, for the first thought in her mind was losing her morning's porridge. So she snatched the club from the goblin's hand and off she took after him.

Now the goblin had met many a man in that mill by night, but never before in all his days had he met a woman like the lass. He didn't know just what to do, for it was a new thing entirely, especially since she had hold of his club. A goblin's wits are never very fast at working so he just backed away.

The lass came after and banged the goblin over his ugly head with the big black club. Into the corners and out again she drove him, and round and round the mill, and sometimes she hit the goblin and sometimes she hit the wall, but all of it made a fearful sort of a racket.

The miller slammed the house door to, and he and his wife and all they put their hands up over their ears to shut out the terrible din!

And then the goblin came up alongside the hopper where the

139

grain was poured down. Against the hopper there was a big
oaken bar. The goblin just turned his back for a minute so as to
take up the bar, and the lass came up close and planted her
foot in the middle of the goblin's back and gave it a monstrous
shove. Into the hopper headfirst went the goblin, and the lass
turned the mill wheel on!

So there was the goblin between the mill stones, going round and round and round! It didn't kill him, for nothing can kill a goblin, but it hurt him awful bad.

"O-o-o-o-o-o-ow!" shrieked the goblin. "Let me out! Let me out! Let me out!" And he shrieked so loud it all but lifted the roof clear off of the mill. The miller and his wife and all were that frighted that they crept under their beds and pulled their pillows down tight over their ears. But even then they could hear the noise.

"Let me out!" screamed the goblin.

"Stay down there!" called the lass, as she wiped her face and settled her skirts, for the fight had been a hot one. " 'Twill do you good!"

"Oh let me out," begged the goblin, "and I promise you I'll go away and bother you no more."

"You will, then?" asked the lass.

"I promise you I will," said the goblin.

"Well that's worth considering," said the lass.

She shut off the water. The mill wheel stopped turning, the goblin stopped screeching, and all was quiet. But the goblin didn't come up. So the lass reached down, and she caught hold of him by the neck, and she drew him up out of the hopper.

Never was there seen, since the beginning of time, such a terribly used-up goblin. He said not one word, but limped out through the door of the mill and never again was he seen or heard of in those parts.

The lass shouldered her sack of meal and took the goblin's club under her arm and the key and the lanthorn in her hand. She went out of the mill and locked the door and went across to the miller's house. She knocked on the door there for a long, long time before the miller got brave enough to open it. But at last he crept down the stairs and opened it a wee crack.

"Here's your lanthorn and here's your key," said the lass. "I've ground my meal and I've got rid of your goblin for you. And now I'm going home!" And home she did go, with the club and the sack of meal.

By the time she'd made her porridge in the morn the news was all over the village about how she'd driven the goblin out of Lachie's mill.

Lachie had risen early and told the tale all over the country-side. It was at the blacksmith's shop, where he'd stopped in to get a bit of mending done, that Wully the weaver's son heard about it. His heart ached inside of him, for he had been thinking that maybe the lass would change her mind some day about wanting a man to fend for her, and maybe if she did, he'd be that man. But that was when her being afraid of naught was just a lot of talk. But what he'd heard at the blacksmith shop looked like proof that the talk was true enough.

"Och," he said sadly, " 'tis sure she'll never be needing me now." He started up the road very slowly, one foot then t'other. But when he came where the road went into the forest, he heard something that made the hairs of his head stand straight up and he began to run. Because it was the lass's voice, and she was screaming at the top of it! Maybe it wasn't as loud as the goblin screamed, but it was close to that.

"It must be a band of robbers has got after her, and they're killing her," panted Wully, as he raced up the road toward her farm. He came to the dooryard and rushed in, picking up a big club that lay by the gate as he ran.

He threw the door open and took a stand, ready to battle

142

whoever was there, no matter how many! And then he stopped!
There was the lass, standing upon the table between the porridge
bowl and the bowl of milk, holding her skirts to her knees and
screaming for help with her eyes tight shut! And playing around
on the floor below was a wee brown mousie.

143

Wully set the club down and leaned against the doorpost. He let her scream a little bit longer and then said, "They've been telling me you're the lassie that nothing could fright."

The lass opened her eyes and cried to him, "Och Wully, put the beastie out! The dog's gone into the woods and the cat's off in the fields, and there's nobody here can save me but you!"

"Happen you need a man to take care of you after all," said Wully.

"Happen I do!" sighed the lass.

So he took the broom from behind the door, and he drove the wee beastie out of the house.

Then he jumped the lass down from the table, and took her in his arms and kissed her. "We'll be married o' Sunday," said Wully.

"Aye," said the lass, and she laid her head on his shoulder as if that was where it belonged.

So married they were, and happily, too. But whenever she had a bit too much to say for herself, Wully would just say "mousie!" And then she'd grow rosy red and hang down her head, and have no more to say. With all so well understood between them 'tis no wonder that they lived happily ever after.

—FROM *Heather and Broom, Tales of the Scottish Highlands*
BY SORCHE NIC LEODHAS

The Organ Recital

On Saturday morning after her big sister and brother left for the day, Jane Moffat secretly tied a sign on the elm tree near the street, announcing that one of the Moffats would give an organ recital at two o'clock. For the past week, since Mrs. Price had given them her very old little mahogany organ that had not been played for years, all four Moffat children had pumped the pedals hard, playing steadily. Even little Rufus stood on a pedal to pump. Jane wanted to play at her surprise recital music that would shake people out of their seats; and, as soon as Mama went out, she would practice. What happened at the recital is told in the book The Middle Moffat, *by Eleanor Estes, which is filled with hilarious Moffat happenings.*

At last, however, Mama put on her hat and gloves and went to town to buy the week's provisions. Then Jane tried the crashing music for all she was worth.

Rufus tore from the house bellowing, "Criminenty, Jane!" And he didn't come back until it was time for lunch.

"He really doesn't appreciate music," thought Jane. "But then, he's awfully little," she excused him.

To tell the truth, though, Jane herself was far from satisfied with her playing. Even with no one around she could not get that swelling effect that she wanted. Also the right pedal had taken to giving a rasping gasp every time she brought her foot

145

down on it. Feeling tired, Jane sat back and let the music thunder and swell only in her head. She decided not to practice any more, but to keep the music in her head this way and then just crash it out at two o'clock.

When Rufus came home for lunch she asked him to help her with the chairs.

"Who's coming?" he asked.

"Well, I don't know yet. But probably plenty of people will, with that sign out there."

Rufus helped Jane arrange the dining room chairs in a semicircle. Then Jane picked some daisies in the lot across the street and these she put in tall jelly glasses on the small hinged trays at either end of the organ. Next she put on her best white piqué dress. She begged Rufus to put on a clean sailor suit. This he absolutely refused to do. Saturday was Saturday.

"Well, at least you can wash your face," begged Jane. Rufus did not want to do this either, but Jane caught him with the wash cloth and got the worst smudges off.

Now it was nearly two o'clock. She had been so busy she had not been thinking about the music. She hoped it would swell through the house in the proper way, banging against people's ear drums. She wondered if there would be chairs enough for the audience. Supposing hundreds came like at Woolsey Hall? If they did, they would have to sit on the long green lawn.

The idea of hundreds coming made Jane suck in her breath. Stage-struck! That's what she was, stage-struck.

She went to the window and lifted the curtain, hardly daring to look. Were the crowds arriving? No—nobody was coming. She should have made lots of signs and put them in store windows and on the bulletin board in front of the Town Hall.

Nobody was going to come, she thought. But as she was thinking this, she saw Clara Pringle and her little brother, Brud. Clara looked at the sign on the tree and then straggled up the walk, dragging Brud along. Brud looked as though he had been crying. Tears were in his eyes.

Jane met them at the door.

"We come to the show," said Clara.

"There isn't any show," said Jane. "This is goin' to be an organ recital."

"All right then," said Clara, "here's my pins."

She emptied a handful of pins into Janey's palm. In this neighborhood ten pins or one cent was the usual price of admission.

"Does he have to pay?" asked Clara, pointing to Brud, who was standing there looking very miserable.

"No," said Jane. "And neither do you. This is free. Like at Woolsey Hall. Did you ever have to pay to go there?" she asked scornfully, dropping the pins back into Clara's hand.

"Never been," said Clara.

Clara and Brud went into the parlor and sat down together in the big armchair. They squirmed around until they were comfortable and then pulled out their lollipops. Imagine bringing lollipops to an organ recital! thought Jane. Then there was a shuffling step on the porch. My goodness, the oldest inhabitant! The most important person in Cranbury! How nice of him to come! Jane couldn't say one word. He sat down on a corner of the couch and beamed. Jane closed the window behind him so he wouldn't catch cold.

She looked at the clock in the kitchen and found it was just two o'clock. Time to begin. She went to the front window for one

147

last look. It was not good to begin until everyone was seated. But Heavens! Who were all those people? Dozens of ladies, all dressed in white, gathered around the big elm tree, talking, laughing and screaming. "Look, girls," said one, pointing to the sign. " 'Organ recital by one of the Moffats'!"

"Let's go, let's go," they chorused.

"Yes. We have plenty of time," said one.

Now the ladies in white were all coming up the path. With their scarves fluttering in the summer breeze they looked like butterflies. One seemed to be Miss Buckle and one looked like Mrs. Price, but Jane wasn't sure. With so many ladies it was hard to tell.

Jane fled into the dining room, screaming "Mama! Mama!"

But Mama had gone out again. Jane couldn't even find Rufus. And of course Sylvie and Joe had not yet returned. Only Catherine-the-cat was there on the window sill and she looked as though she were saying, "Now see what you've gotten yourself into."

"Oh, oh," groaned Jane, hearing the steps on the porch. She could flee, run out the back door, and pretend it was all a joke. But could she? No. The honor of the Moffats forbade this. What would the oldest inhabitant think? He might never speak to her again. Besides how could she ever look Clara Pringle in the face again? She had said organ recital. So all right then, organ recital.

Jane opened the screen door. Miss Buckle—it was Miss Buckle —stepped in first.

"Hello, Jane," she said with a brisk smile, "we are the ladies of P'fessor Fairweather's Browning Society on our annual outing. We see there is an organ recital today. So—here we are."

To those behind her she said in the crisp way she had of talking, "This is Jane Moffat—the middle one."

"Oh!" said the ladies, the ones in back standing on tiptoe to get a look at Jane. "Well, is it time for the concert?"

"It's not a concert," said Jane, "it's an organ recital."

"I see," nodded the ladies. "Is it time for that then?"

Jane nodded her head slowly and the crowd came in. Jane thought to herself, "I should have had an usher."

The ladies arranged themselves around the room, on the porch, and some out on the lawn, sitting on their handkerchiefs to keep from getting grass stains. While they were so arranging themselves, the oldest inhabitant beamed and nodded his head. Brud Pringle watched him fascinated and offered him a lick of his lollipop.

Jane sat down to play.

Miss Buckle said, "Hush, girls," and everyone grew still.

Jane, too, remained silent and motionless. Perhaps she was dreaming. But a glance through her lashes out of the corner of her eye convinced her there really were lots and lots of ladies all over the place. Organ recital! Music! Bach! Words that no longer had any meaning for her raced through her head. She finally raised her hands to the keyboard. She began pumping hard and desperately with her feet, hoping it would be like Julius Sampson at Woolsey Hall when the first powerful notes shook the audience. However, she was not really one bit surprised when she recognized the first few notes as those of "My Country, 'Tis of Thee." Each note was accompanied by a breathless wheeze from the tired pedal.

The first few notes though were all anyone was destined to hear. For, as Janey pumped down on the pedals with might and main, they gave one loud gasp, and then with a plaintive, whishing noise, like air going out of a rubber balloon, they slumped to the floor, exhausted, defeated by a week of Rufus' rapid one-foot pedaling, and by Jane's own passionate outbursts. Anyway, there they were, flat on the ground, and though Janey conscientiously dug at them with her toes to bring them up again, it was useless. They would not rise again. To tell the truth, Jane was really relieved. However, she was too embarrassed to turn around.

"It's broke," she murmured.

"Oh, what a pity," said Miss Buckle. "We shall . . ." But what Miss Buckle was going to say, no one ever knew. All of a sudden from out of the open places over the sunken pedals fluttered a horde of moths. They had been hatching for some time in the felt linings of the organ, and now they all took flight. There

seemed to be thousands of them. The ladies screamed. They covered their ears and held onto their heads, while the moths fluttered blindly about. The oldest inhabitant just sat and beamed, blowing them out of his whiskers now and then. Brud Pringle tottered around the room trying to catch them in his sticky hands. Catherine-the-cat with a gleam in her eye leapt from chair to table pursuing the fluttering moths. Jane didn't know what to do. She wished she had a butterfly net.

"Oh, oh, oh! Run, girls, run!" screamed one of the ladies and they all made for the door, with moths settling on their hair-nets and even getting down their necks. "Save me!" cried Mrs. Price, banging through the screen door. And all the ladies rushed from the house, followed by a stream of the fluttering moths. Fortunately Mama was coming up the walk.

"What's going on?" she asked in amazement.

Without waiting for an answer she tried to restore order.

"Shoo! Shoo!" She waved her gloves at the moths. Some of the ladies helped by swishing their scarves but most of them ran around in circles, fingers in their ears and eyes tightly closed. Mrs. Price ran and hid in the honeysuckle bush. Jane shooed the moths off the oldest inhabitant although he said not to bother. He didn't mind them. They didn't bite.

Gradually, the moths disappeared. Mrs. Price hesitantly emerged from the honeysuckle bush. But every now and then one of the insects would fly out of somebody's sleeve or scarf and there would be more squeals and screams.

"Now," said Mama when she learned what had happened, "everybody sit down quietly and we'll have some home-made grape juice." She didn't like to have people flee from her house. She thought grape juice would make up for it. The ladies sat down. They shook their clothes and patted their hair. Then suddenly they all began to laugh. They screamed and shrieked now with laughter. Jane had heard ladies laugh like this when she went past a house where there was a party. It had never happened before at the Moffats' house though. Tears rolled down Miss Buckle's chubby cheeks. Even Mrs. Price smiled wanly.

While they were sipping their grape juice and laughing merrily, Rufus rode up on his scooter. A party! When Jane told him about the moths, he was sorry he hadn't been there. He might have collected enough to make his own exhibit case of them for nature study.

The oldest inhabitant was the first to leave. He looked all right still and none the worse for the experience, thought Jane.

"Thank you, mysterious middle Moffat," he said to her as he

shuffled down the path. "It was really better than pulling rabbits out of sleeves."

Jane smiled at him. Mysterious or middle or both, she and he were still friends. That was good.

The Pringles left next, covered with ginger-snap crumbs. And when all the ladies of the Browning Society finally fluttered down the path, with a few last moths hovering behind them, Jane sat down on the top step of the porch munching a ginger-snap. If she wanted to give any organ recitals, she thought, she would have to study and study and study and study. Otherwise, all that would come out when she sat down to play would be "My Country, 'Tis of Thee" with two fingers at the most, and you couldn't hope to shake people out of their seats with that.

Unless, of course, the organ was full of moths, like this one.

—ADAPTED BY MILDRED CORELL LUCKHARDT
FROM *The Middle Moffat* BY ELEANOR ESTES

More Stories to Read or Tell

The collections listed below offer a treasury of stories, and your local librarian will be able to suggest even more. In addition, the copyright page of *Funny Stories to Read or Tell* shows the names of collections or other books from which the material in this anthology was chosen.

Andersen, Hans Christian. *It's Perfectly True: And Other Stories.* Tr. by Paul Leyssac. New York: Harcourt Brace Jovanovich, 1938.

Arbuthnot, May H. *The Arbuthnot Anthology of Children's Literature.* Rev. ed. New York: Lothrop, Lee & Shepard, 1971.

Asbjornsen, Peter C., and Moe, Jorgen. *Norwegian Folk Tales.* New York: Viking Press, 1961.

Ausubel, Nathan. *A Treasury of Jewish Folklore.* New York: Crown Publishers, 1948.

Bleecker, Mary N. *Big Music or Twenty Merry Tales to Tell.* New York: Viking Press, 1946.

Boggs, Ralph S., and Davis, M. G. *Three Golden Oranges and Other Spanish Folk Tales.* New York: David McKay Co., 1936.

Cathon, Laura E., and Schmidt, Thusnelda. *Perhaps and Perchance, Tales of Nature.* Nashville: Abingdon Press, 1962.

_____. *Treasured Tales: Great Stories of Courage and Faith.* Nashville: Abingdon Press, 1960.

Chase, Richard. *The Jack Tales.* Boston: Houghton Mifflin, 1943.

Chekhov, Anton. *Shadows and Light.* Tr. by Miriam Morton. New York: Doubleday & Co., 1968.

Child Study Association of America. *Castles and Dragons: Read-to-Yourself Fairy Tales for Boys and Girls.* New York: Thomas Y. Crowell, 1958.

Colum, Padraic. *The Arabian Nights.* New York: The Macmillan Co., 1964.

154

————. *The Golden Fleece and the Heroes Who Lived Before Achilles.* New York: The Macmillan Co., 1962.

————. Also many other collections.

Cothran, Jean. *With a Wig—with a Wag and Other American Folk Tales.* New York: David McKay Co., 1954.

Courlander, Harold, and Herzog, George. *The Cow-Tail Switch and Other West African Stories.* New York: Holt, Rinehart and Winston, 1962.

Davis, Mary Gould. *A Baker's Dozen.* New York: Harcourt Brace Jovanovich, 1930.

de la Mare, Walter. *The Magic Jacket.* New York: Alfred A. Knopf, 1962.

————. *Tales Told Again.* New York: Alfred A. Knopf, 1959.

Gruenberg, Sidonie M. *Favorite Stories Old and New.* Rev. ed. New York: Doubleday & Co., 1955.

Hatch, Mary C. *Thirteen Danish Tales.* New York: Harcourt Brace Jovanovich, 1947. Also in paperback.

Haviland, Virginia. *Favorite Fairy Tales* (series of 14 books of tales told in different lands). Boston: Little, Brown.

Hazeltine, Alice I. *Hero Tales from Many Lands.* Nashville: Abingdon Press, 1961.

————. *Just for Fun.* New York: Lothrop, Lee & Shepard, 1948.

Jacobs, Joseph. *More English Folk and Fairy Tales.* New York: G. P. Putnam's Sons, 1904.

Kipling, Rudyard. *Just So Stories.* Available in several editions.

Luckhardt, Mildred Corell. *Spooky Tales About Witches, Demons, Ghosts, Goblins, and Such.* Nashville: Abingdon Press, 1972.

————. *Spring World, Awake.* Nashville: Abingdon Press, 1970.

————. *Thanksgiving: Feast and Festival.* Nashville: Abingdon Press, 1966.

————. *Christmas Comes Once More.* Nashville: Abingdon Press, 1962.

Milne, A. A. *The House at Pooh Corner.* New York: E. P. Dutton, 1961. Also in paperback.

Nic Leodhas, Sorche. *Ghosts Go Haunting.* New York: Holt, Rinehart and Winston, 1965.

Palmer, Robin. *Dragons, Unicorns and Other Magical Beasts.* New York: Henry Z. Walck, 1966.

Picard, Barbara L. *The Mermaid and the Simpleton.* New York: Criterion Books, 1970.

Pyle, Howard. *Pepper and Salt: Or Seasoning for Young Folks.* New York: Harper & Row, 1913. Dover Publications (paperback).

————. *The Wonder Clock.* New York: Harper & Row, 1915. Peter Smith.

Stoutenburg, Adrien. *American Tall-Tale Animals.* New York: Viking Press, 1968.

Tashijian, Virginia. *Juba This and Juba That.* Boston: Little, Brown, 1969.

Guides to Storytelling

Here are some suggestions of important books and pamphlets that will help with storytelling or story reading. Many may be found in your school library or public library.

The Art of the Story-Teller by Marie Shedlock. 3d ed. New York: Dover Publications, 1961 (paperback).

Folk Tales Around the World. Reprint from *Compton's Encyclopedia*. Encyclopaedia Britannica Educational Corporation, 425 N. Michigan Ave., Chicago, Ill., 60611.

For Storytellers and Storytelling: Bibliographies, Materials and Resource Aids. The Storytelling Materials Survey Committee, Children's Services Division, American Library Association, Chicago, Ill., 60611. 1968.

How to Tell a Story. Reprint from *Compton's Encyclopedia*. Encyclopaedia Britannica Educational Corporation, 425 N. Michigan Ave., Chicago, Ill., 60611. Written for *Compton's Pictured Encyclopedia* by Ruth Sawyer.

Once Upon a Time. 2d ed. Children's and Young Adult Services Section, New York Library Association. Mrs. Augusta Baker, Director of Children's Services, The New York Public Library, 20 W. 53rd St., New York, N.Y. 10019.

Stories, A List of Stories to Tell and to Read Aloud. Compiled by Ellin Greene. The New York Public Library, New York, N.Y. 10018. 1965. An annotated list plus a subject index by country, heroes, and festivals, and a short list of recordings.

Stories to Tell, A List of Stories with annotations. 5th ed. Ed. by Jeanne B. Hardendorff. Enoch Pratt Free Library, Baltimore, Md., 21201. 1965. Includes a subject list of stories, suggested programs, and a list of poetry collections.

Stories to Tell to Children. 7th ed. Ed. by Laura Cathon et al. Carnegie Library of Pittsburgh, Pittsburgh, Pa. 15200. 1960. An annotated list of stories.

157

Story Telling New and Old by Padraic Colum. New York: The Macmillan Co., 1968.

The Way of the Storyteller by Ruth Sawyer. Rev. ed. New York: Viking Press, 1962. Also in paperback.

Two films that are very enjoyable and helpful to all who like to tell or read stories to others are:

There's Something About a Story, produced for the Dayton and Montgomery County Public Library, Ohio, by Connecticut Films, Inc., 6 Cobble Hill Road, Westport, Conn. 06880. 27 minutes, 16mm. color. To rent or borrow apply to your nearest educational film source.

The Pleasure Is Mutual: How to Conduct Effective Picture Book Programs. The Children's Book Council, Inc., 175 Fifth Ave., New York, N.Y. 10003.

Index